Along to Presidio

Look for other Western & Adventure novels by
Eric H. Heisner

West to Bravo

Seven Fingers a' Brazos

T. H. Elkman

Short Western Tales: Friend of the Devil

Africa Tusk

Wings of the Pirate

Conch Republic, Island Stepping with Hemingway

Follow book releases and film productions at:
www.leandogproductions.com

Along to Presidio

Eric H. Heisner

Cover Art & Illustration by Ethan Pro

Visit our website at
www.leandogproductions.com

Cover Art & Illustrations by: Ethan Pro
Contact: info@ethanpro.net

Dustcover jacket design: Dreamscape Cover Designs

Hardcover ISBN: 978-0-9995602-6-6

Printed in the United States of America

Dedication

For Adeline:
Grandmother ~ Daughter

Special Thanks

Amber W. Heisner, Richard Curilla
& Gary Hubb

Note from Author

Western films and the history of the American West have always been important influences for me as a storyteller. At an early age, my father introduced me to cowboy movies that used the names of real-life characters and made them into our original super-heroes. From those dime novel tales came names such as Jesse James, Buffalo Bill Cody, Wild Bill Hickok and my father's all-time favorite, Wyatt Earp.

Growing up with westerns, I was always eager to latch on to the historic monikers that were used in films and TV. Years later, researching the true-life experiences of my western heroes, I was disappointed by the fanciful tales and cinematic liberties that Hollywood used to draw in young, impressionable viewers. A film that still bothers me to this day was directed by the master of westerns and has some of the best scenes and acting that ever graced a movie screen.

The story is certainly a classic, but the use of historic names and locations in a fictionalized story makes me cringe. The director claimed to have heard the details right from the source, but today's well-researched audience knows the true west history much better than to believe tales passed along in the early days of motion pictures. As a writer and filmmaker, my goal is to craft a realistic story in a fictional setting that can someday be brought to a movie screen while steering clear of over-used names made famous at a certain corral.

Eric H. Heisner

September 16th, 2019

Chapter 1

The sky is cloudless and blue to the horizon, above the sun-drenched, rock-studded grazing scrubland of the Texas plains. Three middle-aged cowboys on horseback usher a small cluster of longhorn cattle, while, in their dusty wake, another man handles a supply wagon. The ribbed, canvas military-surplus wagon bumps and grinds at a steady pace, as the horseback riders herd the cattle.

A pair of long-legged jack mules lean into the creaking wooden wagon rig and pull easy over the flat, rocky terrain. The eldest of the herding travelers sits atop the wagon box and cradles the set of leather lead-lines loosely in hand. He gives a low clucking with his tongue, flicks his wrist and matches the animals pace in harness. Years of out-of-doors work in the sun show on deep-creased features, accented by grey wisps of hair and a silvery mustache.

Under a pair of thick, shaded brows, he stares forward to the three men in saddle before him. A hint of a prideful grin appears under the long overhanging whiskers, as he watches the riders keep the unruly assembly of wild beasts in check. Long-horned and raw-boned, the maverick collection of beef-on-the-hoof ambles west into the afternoon sun.

~*~

A stagecoach heading in a south-westerly direction rumbles and creaks behind a trotting, four-up team of horses. Traveling on the wagon-rutted path that leads away from the main military road, the passenger and supply transport rolls through the desolate West Texas landscape. The unescapable cloud of churned road dust lingers behind the spoked wheels like a ghostly visage of the traveled trail.

On a steep ridge above the rocky canyon terrain, several cowboys on horseback watch the stagecoach pass by. The ranch foreman of the *D/W* brand, Jenks, stands beside his cow pony with his vest open and britches undone while he starts to urinate. He leans his shirt-sleeved elbow against the animal's flank and stares over the seat of his saddle, down at the moving stagecoach. "Another one... Since Dutch paid 'em, they're coming to town twice a month now."

One of the dust-covered cowboys takes a long swig from a clouded bottle of whiskey and, with his palm, taps the cork back into the opening. He lies back on the saddle cantle and tucks the glass vessel under the flap of his unfastened saddlebag. With a squirrelly eye for mayhem and mischief, Curtis has the vain impression of authority that comes from being the heir to Dutch Werner, the biggest rancher around. "Let's go have a bit of fun with this load of passengers. I'll give the rest of this jug to anyone who can make one of them Eastern Lillies piss their trousers."

Curtis pats the bottleneck poking from his saddlebag, and a rough cowboy on the end of the lineup smiles as he leans over to check his saddle cinch. The others adjust their reins through their fingers and look to Jenks for direction. Stumbling against his horse, Jenks struggles with buttoning his trouser fly as his loosened gun-belt slides below his waist. "Watch yer damn shootin'. The driver won't open up with that scattergun if'n we don't lay any lead into his coach."

Along to Presidio

Jenks adjusts his cartridge belt up and buckles it tight. He pushes his pistol deeper in the holster and reaches high to grip his saddle by the horn. Raising a knee, he steps in the stirrup and swings a leg over the seat before looking sternly at Curtis and the other three mounted cowboys next to him. "And... back at the ranch, no one whispers a thing to Dutch 'bout any of this. Ya hear?"

Curtis flashes a smug grin at Jenks and lets out a whooping yell, as he clenches his spurred heels to his mount's underbelly and urges the steed over the steep lip of the ridge. In a cloud of raised dust, kicked up by skidding legs in loose terrain, he guides his horse toward the valley floor below. Dutifully following his lead, the other cowboys spur their mounts down the precipitous slope in a blur of horses, riders and churned earth.

~*~

The passenger stagecoach rumbles along at an easy lope, as the driver looks out at the rock-strewn surroundings. A drifting haze of trail-dust catches his eye, and he glances to the rim of the valley as several riders come on from the south. The stagecoach driver straightens in the box at the front of the coach and blurts out a mumbled curse. "Sum' bitch... Heeahhh... Get up there!" He violently slaps the leather lines across the sweat-creased rumps of the harness team and, in unison, they break into a loping gallop.

Thick dust churns up from the wagon-trail as the stagecoach's metal-rimmed wheels spin and creak at full tilt. The oncoming cowboys ride up alongside while shooting their pistols skyward, yipping and hollering in an attempt to intimidate the passengers inside. The man in the driver's box looks over at the cowboys and shakes his head in disgust. "Them gol-durned Werner ranch hands think they's bandits."

One of the drunken riders draws his feet from the stirrups, puts them to the leather saddle skirts and tries to stand in the seat while his horse gallops alongside the coach. A jogging misstep of the animal jostles the rider back into the saddle, and he barely recovers his seat as the stagecoach continues down the rutted path. The driver shakes his head unamused and gives another rolling slap of the lead lines to keep up the running pace of the harness team.

~*~

At the north rim of the valley, a set of horseback riders sit astride their mounts and watch the exploits of the pursued stagecoach. They look behind at their uncle driving the supply wagon between the herd and the cliff's edge, then to their younger brother, Ben, coming up alongside to take a gander. The ambling herd of longhorn beeves moves along the high ground of the ridge, walking slow while the horseback men wait and observe as the stagecoach continues to race away. The eldest sibling, Vic, looks over at his brother beside him. "Whatcha think about that Everett... Bandits?"

The middle child of the three Colbert brothers, Everett, strains his eyes to the distance and shakes his head slightly. "Looks to be jest a bunch of wags... Ya see the way that one feller is foolin' on his horse?"

Ben urges his mount up beside his older brothers, and their uncle eases the supply wagon to a halt a short ways back along the ridgeline. The father-figure of the group, Jacque, stands in the wagon box to get a better outlook over the landscape below. With reins in hand, he tips back his wide-brim felt hat and wipes the film of dirt away from his sweated brow. Jacque spits aside and speaks to his horseback nephews, "Instead of watching, shouldn't we be helping 'em yonder?" He observes his youngest nephew line up with the others to watch the chase from their vantage on the ridge.

Everett hesitantly peers aside at his two siblings, then tilts his chin back slightly toward his uncle in the wagon. "Well Jacque, don't really seem to be any of our business." Ben impatiently skitters his horse sideways, seeming eager to ride to the coach's aid, but holds back alongside his kinfolk.

Vic scans the rocky terrain and nods his head contemplating. "If'n that stagecoach keeps up that runnin' pace, there'll be nothing left but an awful wreck if those horses jump the traces on that turn ahead."

~*~

The stagecoach driver gives the lathered harness team another rolling slap of the reins, as he diligently watches the cowboy tricksters shooting their pistols in the air alongside. He looks ahead to the rutted wagon-road before him, as it appears to drop off suddenly and take a sharp turn to the left. Braced in the driver's box, he gathers up a handful of lead-lines, plants his feet firm and pulls back with all his strength. "Whoaaa there... Whoooaa I say!"

Throwing their heads and snorting, the wide-eyed horse team jolts to a slower pace. With lathered cakes of sweat-foam dripping from hide and rattling harness leather, the hitched team nears the curve in the furrowed roadway. The dogging cowboys continue to gallop alongside but refrain from the playful shooting of their firearms at the sight of the impending wreck. Attempting to bring the passenger coach to a halt, the driver hollers ahead to the agitated team of animals. "Whooaa... Easy now."

The creaking stagecoach setup nearly disappears in a cloudy haze, as the trailing trail dust sweeps by and settles. With a cough, the driver grumbles a cursing rant as he finally stops the animal team. The pursuing cowboys ride wide of the bunched up horses kicking at the harness traces and circle the halted stagecoach while firing several pistol shots skyward.

~*~

From their position, high on the far ridge, Vic sits horseback and squints down toward the chaotic scene below. "Hmm... Looks like they ain't gonna have a wreck at least."

Everett glances at his brother and pushes back in the slick-fork saddle. "I would have never stopped that coach."

With a knowing grunt, Vic responds, "Yeah, you'd a ruther run 'er off the edge of a mountain or bungle the team into the rock than tuck yer tail to anyone."

Ben nods his wholehearted agreement and Everett appears surprised at his brother's harsh assessment. "I ain't that hard a case. I would have just slowed the coach down a bit, that's all. No advantage in stopping for them greenhorn road agents."

Standing in the front box of the supply wagon, Jacque peers into valley at the stopped stagecoach in the distance. "You gonna do something or jest stand 'nd talk 'bout it?"

Everett turns in his saddle seat to face his uncle in the wagon. "Nope, we're headed for California. It's none of our concern what happens along this Texas border territory." Pulling his horse back from the overlooking ridge, Everett steers his mount away and follows after the slow moving herd of cattle.

Ben stands in the stirrups and twists to look back at Jacque and then to his eldest brother Vic, who shrugs with uncertainty. The youngest of the siblings sinks down in the saddle and sighs, disappointed. "Well, I guess that's that."

Vic grimaces and notes Everett riding away, trailing the cattle. "Yep, your brother Everett has spoken."

Ben wobbles his head at Vic, while the dust settles around the playful cowboys and halted stagecoach below. "Don't you ever want to argue a point with him?"

"What good would it do?'

Along to Presidio

The pair of siblings ease their mounts back from the ridge, then turn after their brother and the herd of longhorns.

~*~

The intercepted stagecoach remains immobile and the fidgety team of leader horses paws impatiently at the ground. The annoyed driver bends forward and reaches down at his knee to take hold of his short-barreled shotgun, as Jenks quickly rides up to the front of the coach and gives the driver a broad wink. "Jest take 'er easy and no one will get hurt."

The stagecoach driver sits up straight and stares hard at Jenks. He lifts his rein-filled hands then spits the wad of chaw from his cheek to the side. "If it ain't Indians, it's assholes."

Jenks glances at the shotgun propped against the inside of the driver's box. He grabs it by the tip of the double barrel, draws it out and tosses it aside. The ranch foreman holsters his sidearm and adjusts his hat before grinning at the driver. "It ain't worth it… Jest havin' a little fun is all."

The driver seems to relax somewhat, offering a slight nod then turns around to look as the stagecoach is jostled by one of the horseback riders. A cowboy dismounts at the large, rear wheel and pulls open the passenger door. A flash of sunlight shimmers on the nickel-plated revolver in the cowboy's hand, as he motions threateningly to the few occupants inside. "Come on y'all! Git on out o' there!"

A couple of town-dressed gentlemen peek out before climbing down past the cowboy clinging on the hind wheel. They nervously stand outside the perceived protection of the stagecoach interior and gaze up at the horseback brigands. Still mounted, Curtis rides up, peers inside and hollers, "C'mon, all of you. Step out!"

An older, mature woman gingerly descends from the coach and looks to the horseback characters circling around. She gives a sharp rap with her folded fan to the knuckles of the cowhand hanging at the door frame and he yelps as he hops down from his footing on the stagecoach wheel hub. Defiantly looking over at him, she then turns to help escort a young lady down the narrow step.

Visibly stunned, the cowboys stare awestruck at the young beauty as she appears in the stagecoach door frame. Jenks sits back against the high saddle cantle and whistles, "I'll be damned… A desert rose."

One of the cowboys grins wide and smears the backside of his hand across his sparse whiskers to clean the dirt from his face. "Jackpot!"

Tossing his bridle reins to one of the other cowboys, Curtis steps down from his saddle and jauntily walks up for a closer inspection of the disembarked passengers. He studies the town-attired gentlemen, pushes his face uncomfortably close to theirs and breathes out, "Are these here yer women?" The pair of accosted travelers stands nervous and silent. "Yous both deaf?" Whipping his pistol from his holster, Curtis gestures the firearm before the men's faces and taps one of them on the side of the head. "Ya need to clean out yer ears?" With his free hand, Curtis puts a finger in his own ear and gives it a twist. He stares at the two silent men a moment and then barks at them, "I asked if these're yer women!"

The two frightened gentlemen glance over at the older woman, then up at the young lady in the stagecoach doorway. They cower meekly and shake their heads side to side in unison which sends the surrounding cowboys into a fit of entertained laughter. Curtis turns his attention back to the women and approaches the older one standing below the step. "I'll say, yer wrinkled hide don't seem all used up quite yet. You want to come play my Mommy?"

The woman hauls off and gives Curtis a solid slap, pushing his hat off and nearly knocking him to the ground. The cowboys all roar with laughter as the rancher's son reels from the blow and stumbles back. The woman turns away from the pride-injured cowboy and speaks to the young lady, "Get back in the coach, Adeline." The attractive female looks around at the gawping crowd of unshaven faces then begins to return inside the stagecoach.

Curtis recovers from the blow and hollers toward her. "Hold it now! You jest come on down from there, little lady." He steps forward to grasp at Adeline's dress and the older woman gives him another whacking slug to the further entertainment of the observing crowd. The battered cowboy gives the woman a hard shove aside and grabs hold at the bottom hem of Adeline's dress, which rips away as she tries to escape inside the stagecoach.

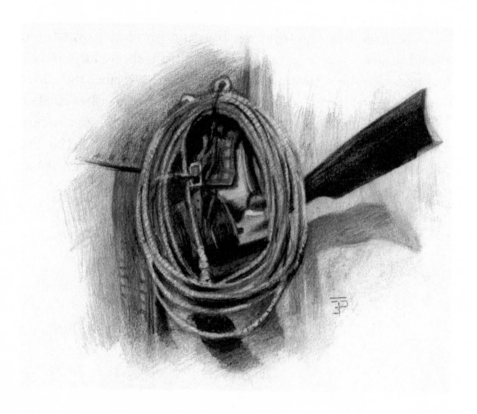

Chapter 2

From the far ridge on the horizon, Jacque sits in the wagon witnessing the scene below. He stands and calls after his nephews as they trail the herd of cattle along the high ground. "There are some womenfolk down there in that stagecoach. They seem to be in need of aid." The three siblings circle their horses and ride back alongside the stopped supply wagon overlooking the valley below.

They all observe, across the distance, as one of the dismounted cowboys reaches into the stagecoach doorway and forcefully grabs at the feet of a female passenger inside. Vic shakes his chin and murmurs aloud to the brothers. "Damn... That sure looks to be out of hand."

Ben nods his agreement as he watches the encounter below and attempts to keep his eagerness at bay. "It sure do."

Taking a seat in the wagon, flexing the springs on the bench, Jacque gazes over judgmentally at his three nephews. "You boys gonna do something about it now?"

Ben tilts his head and looks questioningly aside at his middle brother. "Yeah, that's not right."

Everett stares into the valley and then gazes aside at their uncle. "What do you intend for us to do?"

There is a moment of quiet as Jacque parts his drooping moustache whiskers with his thumb and finger, then spits aside before speaking. "You do what you think is right."

The three brothers stare downward to the unruly behavior at the stagecoach, and Everett turns in the saddle to glance back at his uncle. "Will you cover us with that rifle?"

Leaning over, the old timer in the wagon draws a Winchester rifle from the behind the seat bench and levers a metallic cartridge into the breech. "Yep, I surely will."

The saddle mount nearest to the wagon shies from the sound of the cocking rifle and Vic gathers up a fistful of reins to control his horse. He gazes over to his uncle and grumbles, "Now, don't try to lob too much lead down there, old man. You'd have 'bout as good a chance of hittin' one of us as anything else."

Jacque grins from beneath his long, overhanging lip-whiskers, as he holds the rifle across his lap and pats it fondly. "I'll be sure to hit what I'm aimin' at."

Everett looks to his young brother mounted beside him. "Ben, you comin' with Vic and I?" The little brother draws his sidearm from his gun-belt, cocks it halfway and rolls the revolving cylinder along his shirt sleeve. He stops with the empty chamber below the loading gate and goes to pull a sixth round from his cartridge belt. Everett tilts his head and instructs his younger brother, "Ben if you cain't do the job with five, you best not get started at it in the first place."

Ben takes his hand away from the ammunition on his cartridge belt and resets the pistol hammer on the empty chamber of the cylinder. He twirls his handgun a few revolutions before dropping it back in the leather holster set high on his hip. With a look toward Vic and a grin to Everett, he takes up the slack in his reins of his eager saddle mount. "Yep, I'll be right alongside yous both."

Everett gives an affirming nod to Vic and they peer over the steep descent of the embankment to the valley below. "Let's get to it then..." He gives the rump of his horse a slap to urge him ahead and Vic follows the middle brother's lead.

Ben holds his mount back and looks to his uncle in the wagon before he gives a departing wave. "See ya, Jacque."

The older man sits with the lever-action rifle across his lap and offers a friendly salute from the wide brim of his hat. "You take care of yourself now, boy." Ben nods and releases the slack on his bridle reins to give his horse plenty of head. With a clench of spurred heels, Ben lunges over the edge of the ravine, following the path of his brothers.

~*~

At the halted stagecoach, Curtis clings to the hem of Adeline's torn dress as she braces herself firmly in the door. The older woman hauls off and repeatedly clubs the vigorous cowboy across his shoulders with her folded parasol, until he kicks out and pushes her forcefully aside to the rocky ground. "Get back from me, you old biddy!" He turns his aggressive attention back to the young woman inside the stagecoach and catches a lingering glimpse of the bared flesh along her calf. With renewed zeal he positions himself on the entry step and tugs lustfully at her leg. "Come here, ya little wildcat."

Curtis grunts and chortles devilishly at the fearful expression in Adeline's eyes, until he receives another smack across his back and shoulders. He groans while shaking it off, turns to the parasol-wielding woman who is reeled back to swing again and kicks out his boot to her exposed midsection. In a gasping ruffle of dress and parasol, the older woman is pushed back against the duo of gentlemen from the coach. Curtis calls to them with a threatening sneer, "Keep that crazy woman back or I'll put a slug of lead into yer bellies." Reluctantly, the two men restrain the struck woman as she tries to regain her breath.

Sliding on her bottom along the floorboards of the stagecoach, Adeline pushes back to the opposite door panel. She stares, horrified, as Curtis faces toward her and slowly crawls inside the open doorway. He flashes a wicked smile and whispers low, "Now honey, I jest want a little sweetness."

Curtis climbs into the stagecoach and Adeline kicks out at him with her heeled boot, connecting with his lower jaw. His head cocks to the side, and he touches blood at his mouth. Sporting a cut lip and blood-smeared teeth, he climbs closer. "I hope you like the taste of it fresh..."

The ill-intentioned cowboy crawls closer and breathes heavy over the recoiling female trapped between bench seats. He looms over her and leans down menacingly, putting his face closer to hers. His hot, whisky-tinged breath burns her eyes and he slowly licks the whisker stubble around his lips. In an instant, his eyes register surprise as someone grips his own ankles and tugs. Astonishment fills his features as he is pulled backwards out through the stagecoach doorway.

Ungracefully dragged from the interior of the coach and tossed to the ground, Curtis takes a moment to recover. He looks up to see several more riders and Everett standing over him with a drawn pistol leveled directly at his forehead. Squirming under the barrel of the gun, the cowboy counts the bullet lead inside the cylinder and then peers around at everyone staring down at him. Embarrassed, yet cautious, Curtis barks, "Who the hell do you think you are?"

Everett growls at Curtis with hard, lethal intentions. "I'm the one who will forever quit you of your misdeeds."

Jenks adjusts his weight in the saddle and covers his open palm over the walnut grip of his holstered sidearm. "Now, don't you harm him mister."

His arm extended with the pistol aim held steady, Everett takes a deep calming breath and looks up and around at the group of observing bystanders and horseback cowboys. He watches as the woman helps Adeline from the coach and comforts her. The team of horses hitched to the stagecoach snorts impatiently in the harness rig and pushes the coach back slightly against the braked wheel. All is intensely still until Everett lowers his pistol aim on Curtis and glares up at Jenks. "You want 'im alive… Then get 'im out of here."

Jenks walks his horse over and peers down at Curtis hunkered in the dirt. "C'mon kid, let's go 'n git."

Curtis scoots on his hindquarters a short distance to the stagecoach wheel, then climbs to his feet. He gazes at Everett, then up to Ben and Vic still horseback, and studies their faces. "I won't forget this… or you three."

Ben nudges his mount forward toward the coach. Already having his pistol drawn and rested against his thigh, he stares down at Curtis. "I should hope not."

One of the mounted cowboys leads an empty cow-pony over, and Curtis grabs the slick-forked horn and swings into the saddle. The leader of the cowboys spits blood from his busted lip and stares at Everett beside him, afoot but standing his ground. Flustered for words, Curtis shakes his head and turns to the others. "C'mon boys, funs all over here… Nothin' but whores and dickless greenhorns to tend with."

Everett reaches up and grabs a hold of Curtis' sleeve, pulling him from the saddle seat and slamming him back to the ground with a puff of dirt. He stares intensely down at the stunned loud-mouth and puts a firm hold to the prone man's upper chest with the spur heel of his boot. Everett narrows his eyes and nearly whispers to Curtis squirming on the ground, "There's no need of any disrespect."

Curtis coughs and clutches at Everett's heel as it digs in and clamps him down near his throat. "Get the hell off me!" Whining helpless he croaks, "Jenks, shoot this son of a bitch."

Everett leans down and puts more weight on his firm-footed hold on Curtis. "You ain't learned much, have ya?"

Curtis tries to push Everett's foot away from the hard-pressing stance as he gasps for breath. "I'm sorry, I'm sorry... Now get off me, dammit!"

Easing off the clamping chest hold Everett looks at the ladies and the pair of gentlemen passengers from the waylaid stagecoach. "I believe you owe these folks an apology." Everett toes Curtis' chin toward the crowd.

"Yes, yes... Git yer damn foot off of me!"

Everett removes his boot and lets Curtis sit upright. The ego-damaged cowboy glares at Everett, then scrambles to his feet and dusts off. He walks back to his horse and lifts a foot in the stirrup while mumbling his words of apology. "Sorry for any offense you might have took from my deeds." Curtis turns to look at Everett who gives an affirming nod, as the dismissed cowboy mounts his horse and jabs his spurred heels violently to the horse's flank.

Jenks waits on his horse as he watches Curtis lope away, then steers his mount nearer to where Everett stands. "We was jest having some fun. Didn't mean nothing by it." Everett stares coolly at Jenks a while, then lets his gaze linger on the two cowboys alongside before he turns away without saying a word. Sensing the obvious insult, Jenks bites his tongue on the matter but appears ill at ease. He tilts his head to the riders beside him and trots off after Curtis.

Everett turns to the stagecoach driver still perched up in the box with the lead lines in hand. He bends down, grabs up the short-barreled shotgun from the ground and blows some of the dust from the receiver. Everett hands the gun up to the waiting driver. "You gonna to be alright from here?"

Along to Presidio

The driver offers a nod and positions the sawed-off shotgun across his lap. "We got quite a few miles ahead yet, but tonight we stop at a stage stop to the south o' here."

Everett glimpses over at the ladies and set of town-dressed gentleman but continues to speak up to the stagecoach driver. "You gonna take these city-folk back to where they come from?"

Everett lets his gaze linger on the younger woman, then turns his attention back as the coach driver speaks, "Nope, will be dropping 'em all at Fort Clark and heading to towns west 'fore I start the loop again."

His attention perked at the mention of a possible town, Vic licks his lips and rubs his hand across the whisker stubble covering his chin. "Ya say there's a town west of here?"

The stage driver swivels on the coach seat and looks over at the horseback figure of Vic. "There's a spit of one a few hours ride west, jest over that set of hills. That route will take ya along to Presidio within the week."

Everett holsters his pistol and puts his hand on the dusty iron rim of the forward stagecoach wheel as he stares up at the coach driver. "Y'all best be git'n on your way then." Everett steps to the side of the open stagecoach door, looks the passengers over and motions for Adeline's hand. "Miss."

She cautiously takes his outstretched hand and lets him help her up into the stagecoach. She gazes down admiringly at Everett as he offers his help to the other woman and aids her as well. With both women situated inside the coach, the two well-dressed male passengers step forward to climb aboard. Everett blocks their path and puts a hard stare on them both. "You fellas have pistols?"

The two men seem embarrassed and uncomfortable as they reply in unison. "Yes... But, uh... We're not gunfighters."

Everett continues to block their path to the open door. He shakes his head admonishingly. "Not a one of us here are. If you call yourselves men, the next time you'd better do a sight more than you done today." The two lower their heads with a feeble bow and Everett steps aside to let them pass by.

After the two gentlemen climb aboard, Everett walks toward his waiting saddle horse. Looking up at his brothers, he lifts his foot to the stirrup and swings into the leather seat. He ventures a glimpse inside the stagecoach at the women benched beside each other as the men get situated.

The appealing vision of the attractive young woman returning his gaze puts a burning sensation to Everett's chest. The fleeting urge to someday settle down, create roots and a home swells over him and he takes a quick, arrested breath. He breaks his gaze from the admiring female and quickly quells the unwanted emotions, as he steers his horse from the striking presence in the stagecoach and trots away.

Inside the coach, the gentlemen nod respectfully to the womenfolk settled opposite and sit back in their former seats. The driver leans over to swing the door closed and Adeline observes the three men riding away. She continues to watch out through the open windows of the stagecoach as it jostles, then rolls forward, and the view of the horseback riders passes from her sight.

Chapter 3

The cool night air of the southwest high desert blows softly through the dancing flames of a campfire. The three brothers sit around the leaping licks of orange fire as Jacque prepares their dinner. Ben pokes another stick into the flames and looks around at his older siblings and uncle. "What do you figure about those fellers we run into today?"

Vic adjusts his back against his saddle gear propped on the dry, sandy ground. "Jest some liquored cowboys out having some rowdy fun. Don't you think, Everett?"

Everett seems lost in thought but breaks from his quiet musings to glance up at his brothers. "Suppose so."

Vic keenly watches his brother and smirks teasingly. "What do you figure about them two ladies? A sight for sore eyes out here in the bushy wilds, eh brother?"

Ben smiles and brightens at the mention of the females. "Kinder makes you want to head to Fort Clark, don't it?"

Jacque wanders over to stir the contents of the cast iron pot hanging by the campfire. With a wooden spoon in hand, he takes a knee and looks around at his youthful nephews. "Yer jest a bunch of young roosters yet. There'll always be other ladies and other towns."

Vic scratches the patches of silvery-gray beard on his whiskered cheek and grins insightfully. "Always others, sure, but I jest ain't all young-looking anymore, like some others."

The oldest brother lobs a small stone high over the campfire at Ben and continues to scratch his bearded chin. "Sure would be enjoyable to visit that other burg, even if it is just a spit of one. The stage driver said it was nearly over that rise."

Ben touches the back of his hand along his young cheek which has a wispy patch of whiskers compared to the others. "Sure would… Been a while since I got cleaned up in a town."

Vic grunts as he kicks his booted feet out to cross them at the ankles and adjusts to get comfortable. "Hell, Ben, I could get one of them sucklin' calves 'n put a bit of teet milk on yer chin. It'll have them few whiskers cleaned up in a jiffy." Grabbing up the tossed stone, Ben hurls it back at Vic.

Jacque stirs their dinner a while, replaces the lid on the pot and stands. He straightens his back and stretches, as he looks down at the men gathered around the camp circle. "Well, I ain't a goin' to town with you three, that's fer sure." The older man smoothes back his moustache with his thumb, "You don't need an old timer taggin' along to ruin yer fun." Jacque looks around at his younger kinfolk and grins wide. "Besides, I've certainly had women enough for my lifetime." He looks to the tickled reaction from his nephews and waves the wooden spoon at them. "Now the only gals who'll pay me any sort of mind are gettin' to be pretty old lookin'."

Kicked back against his saddle gear, with his arms folded on his chest, Everett smiles and calls over to his uncle, "I bet you could still turn the heads of plenty of gals."

Jacque sighs with a nod, "When you mature to my age, the ladies are too soft, too stringy or too costly on the hour." The three brothers gaze up at the time-worn figure, as the firelight flickers over the map of wrinkles across his aged face.

Taking the lid from the pot, Jacque inspects their dinner and waggles the wooden stirring stick at his nephews again. "I'll stay with the wagon and watch over these horny four-legged critters, so you young'uns can give what there is of a town a once over." Jacque gazes around at each of their faces. "Go have some fun and tie one on, 'cause there ain't much else 'tween here and where we're headed." Jacque shuffles back to the cook table at the side of the wagon and leans on the frame. "I'm sure proud of the way you all handled yourselves today. A man could do no better than to have a set of boys like you."

~*~

A blanket of bright stars spreads across the horizon on the breezy, cool night as a dim light comes from a lantern inside a patched-together log cabin serving as a bunkhouse. Jenks and another cowboy sit on the porch, smoking as the rest of the hands play a game of dice on the bunkhouse floor. The shadowed features of the cowboy blows a puff of smoke into the light from the open door as he takes the glowing, hand-rolled cigarette from his lip. He looks over at Jenks, kicked back in a wood chair against the cabin wall, and sniffs, "Ya figure the kid will let today's happenings go?"

Jenks lets the old chair totter against the outside logs. "Nope, don't figure he will. Not in his nature to let someone get the bulge on him."

The cowboy with the hand rolled-smoke pinches it between his fingers and takes another drag. "What sort of payback ya think he has in mind?"

The ranch foreman holds a small clay smoking pipe, clenches the stem between his teeth and lights it as he speaks. "Whatever it is, it will likely be ill-thought out and will cause us a lot of grief."

The other cowboy nods his agreement, tosses the remainder of his smoked cigarette away and shakes his chin. "Why in heck do he always get in a spot to take 'im too far?"

Jenks blows out a cloud of smoke, tilts his head back and stares into the clear night sky. "I surely don't know... Always figured he'd a got himself killed by now, but the lord looks after angels and assholes."

The cowboy nods and kicks his heel in the sandy dirt. "Well, he sure ain't no angel."

~*~

At the outskirts of a no-name West Texas border town, horseback riders approach in the bright, midafternoon sun. The three Colbert brothers ride slowly into the seemingly abandoned town, scanning the empty, barren streets and wind-swept buildings. With Everett riding in the middle and Ben positioned on his right, the trio of riders observe a town that looks to have long since expired. Ben glances around and snorts, unimpressed. "Fine town this is."

Vic whistles low as he looks around, disappointed. "Hell, looks like nobody's even here. Cain't imagine why a coach route would even pass through this way."

The three horseback men travel further down the street past an empty mission church and an adobe marshal's office. Everett nudges his mount ahead and leans down over his horse's neck to peer under the shade of the porch stoop. Glimpsing behind at his brothers, he puts an elbow to the saddle horn and calls out, "Hallo... Anyone around?"

He waits a moment but receives no reply from inside. Everett straightens up in the saddle, turns his horse and looks at his brothers. "Guess there ain't no one here to be found." The creaking of a chair, followed by the scraping of booted feet on a wood-plank floor and a snorting snore, is unexpectedly heard coming from inside the marshal's office. The horseback men in the street observe what appears to be movement in the shadow of the overhanging porch.

At the entryway to the office, a crusty fellow named Polk appears at the door. His eyes narrow at the men as he rubs his left arm. "What kin I do fer you fellas?"

Everett leans down on the horse's neck again and looks the old-time character over. "You the Town Marshal?"

Polk nods and blinks the sleep from his squinted eyes. "I suppose I'm what they refer to as the *Law* hereabouts."

Everett glances at Vic and Ben as they inquisitively nudge their mounts closer alongside him at the hitching post. He turns forward to address the aged lawman positioned in the doorway. "What's the name of this town?"

"Ain't got one."

Vic eyes the marshal strangely. "Why not?"

The disheveled lawman takes a step forward and lets his eyes adjust to the bright daylight. He rubs his chin beard and squints through the midday sun at the unshaven men on horseback in the street. "Nobody stays long... Nobody cares." He looks the three riders over and spits off the boardwalk. "My name is Marshal Polk, and I'm still here 'cause I got no place else left to go."

The wind rattles through loose boards on a building up the street, and Ben speaks out. "Where is everyone else?"

Taking his time to extract a plug of tobacco from deep in his pocket, Polk chews off a wad and stuffs it in his cheek. The marshal sucks in his lips and spits, "Spanish pause."

The three siblings exchange confused looks between each other and Everett straightens in the saddle before asking, "How's that again?"

Polk sucks on the chaw, speaking with his tongue pressed to his cheek. "I said, they's on Spanish pause."

Vic tilts his head at the town marshal, dumbfounded. "We know what you said, but what the hell do you mean?"

Polk stares out at the strangers in the street as if they were from the far side of the world. "I'll put it in plain enough English fer ya – *Siesta*."

The brothers each give the other an amused look and Ben turns to gape out at the empty townscape. "Everyone?"

Marshal Polk nods and spits a stream of brown saliva just past the porch step. "Don't see anyone in the street, do ya? Too damned hot to be out sittin' in the sun like you are."

The heat of midday shines down on them in the street, just to the edge of the shade, and they seem to nod in unison. Vic and Ben absentmindedly wipe the perspiration from their temples and adjust their hats. Everett touches the sweated beard stubble under his chin and peers down at Marshal Polk. "Have you a barber shop in town?"

"Yup."

Vic grunts, "He nappin' too?"

The marshal squints up at Vic with a sarcastic regard. "Go 'n ask 'im yerself. He's there in a building yonder shared with the printing press."

Ben seems surprised. "This town has a newspaper?"

"Has a press, but no one knows how to use it."

Just past the cooling shade of the porch-roof awning, still in the sun, the three brothers remain mounted horseback. Everett adjusts his hat and backs his horse into the street. Realizing they won't get much more information from the freshly awakened town marshal, Everett gives a curt wave. "Thanks for your assistance. Good day to ya, sir."

Vic and Ben watch the old-timer arc his spittle out past the porch stoop, and they wheel their horses around to follow Everett down the street. The seasoned lawman watches the newcomers a long moment, then takes a step back into the shadowed obscurity of the jailhouse doorway. The sound of a wood chair scooting on the plank floor is heard, followed by a set of boot heels thumping on a desktop.

Chapter 4

At the far end of town, the Colbert brothers dismount their horses in front of a building that boasts a combination of barber shop and printing office. Adjusting his hat, Vic looks up at the faded flakes of paint on the sign and muses aloud, "Kinder strange combination."

Everett nods as he climbs the steps to the walkway and his boots scrape the gritty layer of dirt on the wooden surface. He peers through the dirty windows of the unused print shop. "This whole town is a mite peculiar."

Making his way around behind the tethered mounts, Ben climbs the flight of stairs to the planked boardwalk and stomps the trail dust from his boots. He steps up to the printing office/barber shop entrance, gives the wobbly handle a twist and nudges the rickety door aside. "I don't imagine there'll be much of a wait today."

Standing in the cooling shade of the porch overhang, Vic shrugs at Everett and gestures him to follow Ben inside. "After you, little brother." Everett gives Vic a funny look, then gazes down the street and steps into the odd arrangement of barber shop and printing office.

~*~

Dusty haze rises in the wake of six horseback cowboys moving across the open horizon of scrubby, grass terrain. Without slowing their pace, they cut through the milling herd of longhorn beeves, a few miles from the outskirts of town. They angle toward the military surplus wagon with a grazing pair of mules hobbled nearby. The mustached figure standing near the supply wagon reaches behind the bench seat and draws out his lever-action rifle to hold across his chest as he receives the uninvited callers.

As the half-dozen cowboys approach, Jacque makes out the identities of several riders from the previous encounter at the stagecoach. The foraging longhorns bawl as they are forcefully shoved aside and the mounted horsemen fan out in a wide circling pattern around the solitary man at the wagon. The trailing haze of dust settles as the group of bandana-masked riders hold their mounts steady and stare down from obscured features. The leader of the horsemen, with his wild rag pulled high over his nose, moves forward and calls out, "Hey there fella, where's your other pals?"

Backed up against the wagon side, facing the assembly, the older man's experienced eyes narrow and slowly study the gang of veiled riders. Jacque levers a cartridge into the chamber of the rifle and puts the wood stock at his shoulder. "I sure ain't lookin' for any trouble from you cow-hands…" His eyes scan the crowd as he raises the barrel of the rifle. "But I'll accommodate ya, if'n you don't turn tail 'n git."

With the increase of hostility in the air, the sweated mounts flare nostrils, paw the ground impatiently and fidget under saddle. One of the belligerent horsemen moves up, grips his palm to his holstered sidearm and speaks in a muffled tone through his raised bandana. "Yer jest a dry old bean we'll have to teach a lesson to for them others to learn."

Uncle Jacque keeps the long, rifle barrel held upward, lays his finger over the trigger and redirects his aimed sights to the chatty horseman. He drops his grey-whiskered cheek and pursed mustache against the wood of the rifle stock and narrows both eyes to a slit. "What do ya have in mind fellas?" Jacque raises an eyebrow and lets his one eye scan the riders. "In my camp, I don't take kindly to idle threats from young boys hiding behind kerchiefs."

There is a fleeting pause, as the horseback figure stares down at the prepared man standing his ground at the wagon. He looks around at the superior odds in the riders' favor and, with a cautious wave, the horseback leader gestures to the cowboy nearest the canvas-topped wagon. "Burn it down!" The cowboy nods, takes a matchstick from his vest pocket and strikes it across the top of his saddle horn.

As the wooden matchstick smokes and then flares up, the rifleman on the ground quickly turns the aim of his gun. He speaks low and steady. "Blow it out." The cowboy looks to the lead rider and extends his arm with the flaming match out to the canvas topper. A firm squeeze on the trigger and the bullet lead projectile from the rifle shoots the flame from the rider's hand, along with a gory chunk of finger bone.

The severed portion of detached extremity flies through the air and the cowboy yelps as he holds the bloody stub. Reacting in a panic, the other cowboys draw their revolvers and direct them at the lone man backed against the wagon. Jacque quickly levers another round into the rifle chamber. The realization of impending death registers in his eyes just as the empty brass shell casing clatters to the ground.

A long, tense moment passes until one of the cowboys cocks his handgun and fires it at the rifle-wielding defender. A volley of hot, bullet-lead quickly follows from all sides, striking the man at the wagon. A lingering cloud of burnt powder smoke fills the air with a pungent aroma as the deafening echo of gunshots fades. The victim of the shooting drops the cocked rifle and crumples to the dry, dusty ground.

One of the horseback cowboys pushes his way forward, waves his gun and shouts at the riders. "Hold yer fire, dammit! Y'all most likely kilt 'im already!" Jenks lowers the bandana from his face and growls at the lineup of assassins, focusing on one in particular. "Put yer damned guns away!" Curtis laughs through his neckerchief as Jenks hollers at them, "This is not what we wanted."

The cowboys reload the fired pistols and holster them, as the group's contradictory leaders face off with each other. The two lead horsemen circle each other and steer their mounts to the sprawled figure on the ground. The initiator of the violent attack glares at Jenks, lowering his scarf to reveal his recently busted lip. "I'll do a whole lot worse to them others when I get the chance."

Jenks grunts, "This ain't right and you know it."

Curtis twirls his pistol on his finger and drops it into the holster on his hip. "You work for my father and for *me*... So you do what I say until I *make* it right."

Jenks shifts his bandana around his neck and looks down at the shot-up figure of the dying man on the ground. He shakes his head in disgust and looks around at the blank-faced cowboys surrounding the campsite. Jenks wheels his horse away from Curtis and raises his voice for all to hear. "Clear out that wagon, burn it and git them cattle and mule team clear of here 'fore we have more trouble on our hands."

Curtis spools out his rawhide riata and tosses the loop down around the neck of the gun-shot casualty on the ground. Jacque feebly attempts to push the rope off, but Curtis urges his horse backward and draws the rawhide loop ever tighter. Jenks turns and reaches out for the taut rope but misses. "Curtis, what the hell you doing now?"

The rancher's son holds the rope at his side as he backs his horse away a few more steps and drags Jacque along the ground by his neck. "Hell, he's gonna die anyway. Might as well teach them fellers not to mess around in these parts. Curtis looks over at his cowboys with a lethal viciousness. "You know, this is the way pa used to do it."

A sickened look of dread fills the foreman's features, as he appears powerless to diffuse this horrid act of lynching. Jenks draws his horse up alongside Curtis grabs at the rope and tries to speak some sense to his impulsive saddle-mate. "Curtis dammit, that jest ain't needed. You done shot 'im to hell already, that's enough... Now let 'im expire in peace."

Curtis violently jabs his spurs into the belly of his horse and drags the body further along. "Choke yer tongue Jenks! I'm the one who is gonna run this ranch when the old man is gone, so I'm the one who says when enough is enough."

Jenks clenches his jaw and turns away from the ranch owner's son, as the wagon starts to burn and the cattle are ushered away by several riders. The pair of mules kick out against their hobbles, as they move from the flaming wagon. Despondent, Jenks watches as Curtis spurs his horse onward toward the distant town on the horizon, with the limp body of the old man trailing behind in the dirt.

Chapter 5

In an undeveloped patch of real estate behind the print shop, a series of awnings are suspended in the air for shade cover. Beneath the canvas coverings are a setup of bathing tubs, water buckets and a lone barber chair. Vic sits waist deep in a copper washing tub, scrubbing his feet, while Everett sits in the chair with his face lathered up, waiting for a shave.

Seated near a cedar post fence, Ben leans a chair back against the partition, reading an old out-of-date newspaper. Scanning the stories, he turns the brittle pages to the front and reads the headline date. "Hmm, just a few years old..." Everett turns his head slightly and speaks from beneath the shaving foam. "Newspapers are mostly the same whenever."

Stepping out from inside the combination printing office/barber shop, Lonie, the long-haired, whiskered barber, ambles along in the shade of the canvas coverings and casually draws a straight razor from his front apron pocket. He repeatedly swipes the open blade against a leather strop hung on the armrest of the tilted chair and flashes a crooked grin toward his customer. Reclined in the chair, lathered up to his eyeballs, Everett keenly watches the unkempt eccentric sharpen the straight razor. "You do many shaves?"

"Oh, yeah... Some folks come in regular."

Everett takes a deep breath and begins to relax a bit, staring up to the fluttering canvas above. "How often is that?"

"Sometimes twice a month."

Everett keeps his face turned upward but his eyes glimpse sideways toward Lonie as he hones the razor edge. "Leave the mustache."

"Yes, sir."

The long-haired, bearded barber lifts Everett's chin slightly and gently applies the razor. The soft scrape of cut whisker stubble along skin is drowned out by Vic splashing to a seated position in the washing tub. He wipes the film of soap from his shoulders and calls out, amused, toward Lonie. "Why is it, you being the barber 'n all, that you've got hair longer than an Injun and whiskers to boot?"

Lonie squints over at Vic in the tub, as he continues to shave Everett. "No one else in town knows how to cut hair."

Kicked back in the chair against the privacy fence, Ben rattles his newspaper and turns the tan, sun-crisped pages. "It's like the blacksmith that don't fix his own wagon."

Vic splashes the grey, sudsy wash tub water around and laughs while Everett rolls his eyes from the blade near his cheek over toward his older brother. "Hush how 'n let the man concentrate on his task."

"You bet... Looks to be he could use the practice."

The afternoon sun still shines hot on the sunbaked town, and a gentle breeze flaps the fabric awning overhead. Suddenly the sharp snap of a gunshot echoes through the empty street and shatters the peace of the quiet surroundings. Startled at the sound of the discharged firearm, Lonie stands unmoving with a razor full of cut lather and Everett hastily pushes away from him, going over backwards in the chair. Newspaper pitched to the ground and his seat kicked aside, Ben rushes over to his brother. "Everett, are you hurt?"

The shocked barber stands with both arms still raised. He lets his nervous gaze wander from his trembling hand with the sharp blade, dripping shaving lather, to Everett in the tumbled chair with the shaving bib covering over his head. Ben kneels down and helps his brother sit up.

Removing the barber bib from his neck and partly-shaved face, Everett looks to Ben, then over at Vic in the tub. The observing brothers titter, then erupt into laughter, as they take in the unharmed condition of their half-shaved sibling and the shaky, wild-haired barber. Unamused by the incident, Everett picks himself up from the ground and rights the turned-over chair. He touches his close-shaven neck under his chin and looks to Lonie. "Damn, you near slit my throat."

Lonie looks to his still trembling fingers and shrugs. "That's why I say pay first, 'n shavin' always 'fore bathin'."

Ben turns to Vic, who is seated upright in the wash tub. "That settles it... I might just pass on the shavin' part."

Tossing a splash of soapy water toward the younger brother, Vic grins. "Heck, mý offer still goes 'bout puttin' some milk on them whiskers and lettin' a calf lick 'em off!"

Everett shakes off the startle of the unexpected gunshot and settles back into the righted barber chair. He takes a deep calming breath and motions the barber over to finish the job. "You may proceed, Sir." Lonie wipes the dripping lather from the blade and steps forward to continue the task of shaving.

Suddenly another gun blast is heard and one of the empty water buckets is sent skittering across the dirt yard. The four men under the canvas awning pause to gaze at each other, astounded, until another fired shot is heard and a bullet whizzes by overhead. Several more gunshots ring out from somewhere in the street and Vic hunkers down in the tub, sending the cloudy water flowing over the upper rim.

Everett dives from the barber chair and scrunches down behind a row of oak barrels alongside Lonie and Ben. He looks to his youngest brother who draws his pistol out, then over to the barber. "What the hell is going on?"

Innocently, Lonie peers over at the partly-shaved customer and scratches his chin. "Somebody is shooting."

Everett flicks some extra shaving lather from near his nose and turns to his brother. "Where's it coming from?"

Ben gestures with his gun. "Next door, I think."

The barber judiciously wipes and folds the shaving razor and puts it in his apron. "That's Tuck's new place."

Peeking from the cover of the barrels, Ben asks what he and Everett are both thinking. "Who's the hell is Tuck?"

Staying down low, Lonie removes a small, metal flask from his pocket and unscrews the top. "Hollister Tuckburrow. He owns the Barrelhouse."

The nerve-shaken barber takes a swig from the tipped-up flask and is about to take another when Everett stops him. "Put that stuff away. You ain't finished my shave yet."

Lonie pushes long strands of hair back from his face, wags his whiskered chin and replies, "And I ain't gonna finish with some durned fool shooting at us."

Everett gazes over at the copper bathing tub as water sloshes over top of the rim. Bubbles gurgle to the surface through the film of soapy water and a pair of squinted eyes are seen peeking out from below Vic's head of wet hair. Everett grimaces, "This is ridiculous. Vic, you okay?"

The soapy water shifts aside and Vic slowly raises his dripping chin above the water at the rim. "I'm good..."

Ben chimes in. "And clean."

Everett tugs the barber bib from his neck and wipes the remaining shaving lather off his face. He moves to the rear of the print shop building and draws his sidearm from the holstered gun leather hung on a hook by the back door. "Come on, Vic. Bath-time is over."

Chapter 6

On the main through street of the West Texas border town, an interested crowd begins to come out and start to gather in front of the saloon with the sign placard, *Tuck's Barrelhouse*. Everett and Ben come from the alleyway at the side of the barber shop to meet the half dozen gawkers collected around Marshal Polk, who stands in front of them. Everett steps vigilantly into the now-populated street and addresses Polk. "What's going on in there?"

Polk tenderly grips his aching left arm and winces. "Seems to be Melvin Walper is shooting the place up some." Everett looks at the marshal cradling his elbow and inquires, "Are you shot?" The town lawman takes his hand away from his opposite arm, shakes it out, flexes it and wobbles his head. "Nope, just havin' a recurrent pain is all."

With his pistol still at his side, Ben steps alongside the weathered town marshal. "Shouldn't someone stop 'em?"

Polk timidly peeks into the dark interior of the saloon doorway and ponders the source of the offending gunshots. "That's Tuck's place, so it's his business."

The flash from several muzzle blasts erupts from inside the saloon doors and the crowd in the street instantly drops to the dirt. Ben grins at Everett. "Appears, he has reloaded."

On his belly in the street, Everett grimaces as he turns his head to look at Polk. "Where is this Tuck fella anyhow?"

The town marshal moves to a sitting position on the ground, rubs his bothersome left arm and peers down the wide street. "Was down in Mexico, last I heard." Becoming more irritated, Everett scratches his half-shaved beard and glares at Polk. "You're the lawman here. Are you going to do something?"

Polk attempts to avoid Everett's stern gaze and looks around at the questioning faces in the small, gathered crowd. He cradles his sore arm again and stammers, "I wasn't going do anything since my arm has been hurting so god awful... Figured he'd just run out of bullets or get bored with it all." The seasoned lawman looks at Ben, then Everett and rolls his pained left shoulder. "Oh, alright. I'll go in 'n get him."

Polk tugs his old-fashioned, loose-powder pistol from his belt holster, climbs to his feet and ambles across the street. He glances back fleetingly, before he climbs up the few steps and approaches the front double entry. As he cautiously reaches out to push aside one of the partially ajar doors, another gunshot is heard, and a pained expression passes over Polk's features as he spins and crumples to the porch deck.

Squatted next to the others in the street, Everett bends an elbow upward and points his pistol at the building while he thumbs back the hammer. He looks aside at his younger brother and Ben nods, smiling. "Go on 'n get 'im brother."

Everett focuses on the dark entrance. "Aw, hell..."

Dashing across the wide street to the saloon building, Everett holds his firearm ready as he leaps to the low wood-plank porch. He flattens himself against the front wall of the Barrelhouse and cautiously steps toward the collapsed body of Marshal Polk near the doorway. A quick glimpse to the street and the half-shaven brother observes Ben, hunkered in front of the small crowd with his pistol defensively directed toward the saloon doors.

Along to Presidio

Just as Everett approaches the prone lawmen at the front door threshold, the offending gunman, Melvin Walper pokes his head out from the entry to get a better look at the downed marshal. Everett halts as a hat covered head and shoulder protrude from the entrance. He slowly raises his pistol higher, as he takes another step closer to the doorway. As Everett moves closer, the boardwalk creaks softly and startles the intoxicated gunman to attention.

Melvin Walper turns to Everett just as the raised pistol swings down hard, cracking over the drunken man's skull. Groaning, Walper slumps in a heap over the body of Marshal Polk and rolls to the side. The dilated pupils of his whiskey-soaked eyes roll up to the top of his lids and he heaves a heavy sigh as he passes out.

With a fistful of Walper's shirt collar and vest in hand, Everett drags him to the edge of the saloon porch and nudges him over the side. The body drops just below the hitching rail into the dry gutter. Everett gazes out at the assembled crowd now gathering nearer, then looks to his younger brother. "Watch him awhile Ben, and see that he behaves."

Ben steps up with his pistol hanging at his side and stands guard over the drunkard, as he watches Everett return to Polk and kneel down to check him over. The curious crowd clusters in the street fronting the Barrelhouse, and lingers before the wide front porch. A man pushes his way through, climbs the steps and squats next to the body of the lawman. Everett looks to the leather bag the man carries and questions, "You a doctor?"

"Name's Watson... Closest thing to it in this town."

The town dentist lifts Polk's limp arm from the boardwalk and inspects the laid-out form. He shakes his head somberly and feels for a pulse along the dead man's neck.

Everett observes the reluctant physician and wonders aloud, "Is he dead, Doc?"

Watson nods as he continues to inspect Polk's rumpled vest and stained shirt front. "Yup, but not from being shot."

Everett glances over at Doc Watson and murmurs, "What kilt 'im?"

"Guess it was just his time. He don't have any extra holes in him, but he's deader than a post."

The crowd whispers between themselves as Everett stands up and steps away. He descends the few short stairs from the boardwalk and stands next to his younger brother who guards over the knocked-out gunman laid in the gutter. Barefoot, Vic walks around the corner from the alley, with partly damp clothing hastily put on and both boots in hand. He looks to his pair of brothers and then down at Walper. "That the fella shootin' the town up?"

Everett tucks his long-barreled pistol in the waist of his pants and sighs, "Yep." They turn to watch as the doctor stands next to the body of Marshal Polk on the shaded porch.

Doc Watson gently places a hat over the deceased lawman's face and turns to address the gawking spectators "That's all there is to see folks, go home."

The acting doctor steps over to grab the porch support. He nods to the man laid out at the Colbert brother's feet, under the lip of the boardwalk. "That there is Melvin Walper." With the momentary excitement in town over, the crowd begins to disperse and Everett puts out the obvious question. "Hey Doc, what are you gonna do with him?"

The gathered observers drift away to search for shade as the doctor offers a meager shrug. "He'll jest sober up there, I guess, and be okay tomorrow."

Everett looks past the doctor to the dead lawman on the saloon porch. "Yeah, but he surely won't."

Doc Watson looks behind at Polk and nods unhappily. "We got a Chinaman in town who can bury him."

Standing next to his brothers, Everett gazes down at the unconscious drunk at their feet. "Who's gonna hold this one accountable?" The doctor stares at the three remaining men still standing in the street and seems stumped. "For what?"

Everett shakes his head as he looks away from Walper. "Ah, nevermind."

The doctor picks up his unopened leather satchel and asks timidly, "I don't suppose you want the job of marshal?"

Vic and Ben step away with eyes cast downward. Everett peers up at the physician and states firmly, "No."

"How about any of your friends there?"

The brothers exchange unenthusiastic glances between them and Everett shakes his head, replying, "Not a one of us. We're just passing through on our way to California."

The street has emptied of onlookers and Everett jabs a pointed finger at Lonie, who stands at the corner of the building with the printing press, combination barber shop. "Let's finish up what we started so we can get out of here."

Vic looks down at his bare feet and shrugs. "I'm 'bout as bathed as I'm gonna get."

Everett rubs his half-shaven face and waves his brothers along as he strides away. They follow after him and the reluctant barber toward the back, canvas-covered alley.

From dust-shrouded windows, several curious faces continue to peek out at the doctor and two laid out bodies in front of Tuck's Barrelhouse. Doc Watson clutches his small leather medical bag and walks away toward his dental office. In the late afternoon sky, out past the line of buildings on the far horizon, a small plume of smoke drifts upward.

Chapter 7

The late day sun has moved down to the wide horizon as the Colbert brothers ride to the outer fringe of the border town. The limbs of a solitary tree arch from the dry ground with the dark form of a body hung by the neck from a lower bough. The three brothers halt their mounts and stare at the shot, dragged and lynched corpse of their brutally murdered uncle. They are gravely silent, having no words to express the emotions evoked by the ghastly sight.

Eventually, Everett swallows the lump in his throat and nudges his horse forward as he draws his knife blade from the sheath at his hip and cuts the lifeless form down from the tree. The body sags to the ground in a heap, and Everett stares at the loose end of the rope still dangling. He chokes back strong emotions and turns around to look at the small town just beyond his two brothers on horseback.

A tap of his heel sidesteps his mount away, and Everett stares down at the grotesque appearance of his slain relative. A burning rage begins to boil up inside him, as he hoarsely calls out to his brothers standing by. "Tidy him up for burial." Vic steps down from his mount and unfastens the blanket roll from behind his saddle cantle. He walks under the hanging tree and unfurls the woolen covering to drape over the body.

Ben takes a sorrowful breath, wipes away a glistening tear and waits on his elder siblings for further instructions. Still in the saddle, Everett takes up his reins and turns his horse to face the others. Without uttering another word, Everett rides past them both, heading back into town. Standing over the body of their uncle, Vic speaks quietly, "Where you going, brother?"

"I'll be back after a while."

His hand over his holstered sidearm, Ben aggressively turns his horse to follow. "What are you going to do Everett?"

Everett halts his mount just past his young brother and tilts his chin toward him without looking back. "Stay with Vic. I have to attend to things and I'll be along to get you both."

Staying put, Ben watches Everett ride into town and calls out after him, "There's no law in that damned town!"

His voice, choked with devastating emotion, is almost carried away by the afternoon breeze as Everett responds, "There will be..."

~*~

The soft clinking of whiskey glasses being filled and beer mugs thumping on wood tables and scooting on the bar-top comes from the dimly-lit interior of Tuck's Barrelhouse. The saloon is sparsely occupied with the exception of a few folks playing hands of cards at a table and the local rancher, Dutch Werner, with some of his hired hands lined at the bar. Marlow, the bartender, serves another round of drinks and collects the coins tossed on the freshly swabbed plank slab.

Dutch waits for the bartender to finish and move along to the other end of the bar before he turns to his cowhands. His stern look settles upon his two top men, Jenks and Curtis as he spits a stream of tobacco into the cuspidor at his feet. "That sonuvabitch, Tuckburrow." The rancher's tough gaze travels along the lengthy stretch of bar to each of his cowboys. "I'm gonna kill him next time I see 'im."

Anxiously shifting his full beer glass on the bar top, Jenks clears his throat and speaks, "We ain't for certain, 'xactly, it was him, Dutch." The ranching kingpin snarls at the very thought of someone interfering with the local monopoly of his cattle business.

"The mere coincidence makes my gut burn," Dutch's wayward son, Curtis pipes in after he takes another drink from his whiskey glass. "It must have been him 'n those sneaky Mexes he runs with that grabbed all them beeves."

Dutch tips his chin and pours a drink from the bottle. "He gone in and stole them cows right from under our noses." He puts the bottle down with a solid thud and growls aside, "Now that saloonkeeper trash is down in Mexico selling stock that was grazed on our land." He lifts the glass tumbler to his mouth, tosses back the warm whiskey contents and wipes the driblets from his silvery lip whiskers. "Hollister Tuckburrow has been a burr under my saddle fer much too long…"

Jenks puts his elbows to the bar rail, glimpses around the room and holds his drink near his mouth. "Eh, Dutch… You want us to wait in town for him for when he gets back?"

Curtis looks over and half-whispers so that everyone in the saloon can hear, "We could dry gulch 'im easy."

Dutch Werner gives his progeny a cold stare and gazes around the near-empty saloon. "No, there will be none of that. We'll wait for a better time to get even with Tuck."

The cattle boss pours himself another glass of whiskey, as Jenks fiddles with his beer mug and appears concerned. The ranch foreman leans to his boss and speaks in a low voice. "What should we do about that fella and the cattle we found?"

The rancher swirls the amber contents of his whiskey glass and shifts his menacing gaze to his son. "What the hell's a matter with you, Curtis? If that fella you used as a shootin' puppet had kin somewheres, they's gonna want answers."

Curtis instantly withers under his father's stern glare. "It was jest an accident is all it was."

Dutch raises his hand as if to strike down his son, then changes his mind and turns his gaze to focus on his foreman. "Dammit, Jenks... Yer supposed to keep this dunderhead out of trouble. Takin' shots at some driftin' passersby and burnin' wagons is the kinder crap yer supposed to keep 'im clear of."

Curtis drinks, straightens up and tries to justify his act. "All the shootin' was a mishap. He shot first. We was just blowin' some steam, 'n he rifled Jimmy's finger off."

Dutch turns to face down his sniveling offspring. "Blowin' steam from what exactly? Lettin' Tuckburrow make you look like a bunch of jackasses?"

Jenks shoots a scolding glance toward Curtis, hoping to keep him quiet and interjects, "The old fella with the wagon was a crack-shot with a rifle and the boys overreacted some."

Dutch nods, takes another drink then looks sidelong at Jenks. "They overreacted with enough bullet lead to kill 'im. Be sure to make it known it was the doings of that Mexican trash that Tuckburrow hangs with if anything comes of it."

Curtis finishes off his glass of whiskey and slides the empty vessel over in front of his father, hoping for a refill. "What do you want me to do now, Pa?"

Dutch looks at his wayward son and flips the offered glass over on the bar top. Disgusted, he swipes the empty whiskey glass aside, replenishes his own drink and glowers at Jenks, then at Curtis. "Keep yer mouths shut and let it pass."

Chapter 8

The nighttime exterior of the building that houses Tuck's Barrelhouse is lit with oil lanterns that waver with a flickering orange glow from each side of the windowed entry doors. Everett steps up onto the boardwalk flanked by his brothers, Vic and Ben. They take a quick glimpse through the clouded glass panes at the positions of the occupants inside before opening the saloon doors and entering.

With a calm definite stride, Everett moves purposefully across the room to take up a position next to Jenks at the bar. He puts his hand to the smooth wood surface of the slab top, and the bartender saunters over, offering a friendly nod. "What'll you have this evening, stranger?"

Everett rubs his hand along his freshly shaved cheek and gestures to his accompanying brothers, as they push up to the bar beside him. "We'll have three mugs."

At the familiar tone of Everett's recognizable voice, Jenks startles involuntarily and glimpses over at the three. Dutch notices the peculiar reaction from the ranch foreman, leans forward and peers around Jenks. "Hello there, friends... Ain't seen you here around town before." Everett turns his attention to the seasoned rancher and his son, both on the other side of Jenks. The bartender draws the refreshments from a barrel keg and glances over his shoulder with interest.

Dutch puts his hand to Jenks' shoulder and firmly backs him away from the bar rail a few steps so he has a better vantage on the newcomers. "You fellas new to the territory?"

Everett turns his stare forward and gives a nod. "Yep."

Situated behind Dutch at the bar, Curtis looks at Jenks with a frightful, panicked expression, and the foreman subtly shakes his head in an attempt to calm the rancher's son. Curtis hastily places his hand over the handle of his pistol, and Jenks attempts to hold him with a stern glare. For the moment, Curtis keeps his gun holstered and doesn't draw.

Casually, Dutch perches both elbows on the bar top, takes a sip of whiskey and studies the recent arrivals in town. He observes the used wear of their dusted trail-clothes and notices their freshly barbered features. The sharp-eyed rancher pours himself another drink and sets the whiskey bottle down with a thud. "Can I offer you fellas a drink?"

Everett watches as Marlow places the filled glasses of beer before them on the bar slab. The meager foam at the top slides over the mug's rim and puddles on the wooden surface. The three newcomers stare at their poured drinks and remain unnervingly silent, so Dutch raises his own as he continues, "The name's Dutch Werner. This here is my ranch foreman, Jenks and my boy, Curtis."

Everett turns his hard stare directly to Dutch without even a sideways glance to acknowledge Jenks or Curtis. "We've already met."

Momentarily caught off guard by the stern reaction, Dutch appears stunned but quickly conceals it. A quick glance over to his ranch foreman receives an obvious look of guilt. "Now, where would that have been?"

Everett wraps his hand around the beer mug and lifts it to take a mouthful. He peers over the frothy rim at Dutch and takes a slow swig. Lowering the mug of beer to the bar again,

Everett's intense gaze sweeps over to Jenks then at Curtis. "There was something of an unscheduled stopover on the stagecoach route and we crossed paths."

Dutch nods and ponders briefly as he studies Everett and the pair of brothers standing behind him. "Is that so?" The rancher steals another glance at Jenks who nods and then he returns his focus to Everett with a change of demeanor. "You fellas staying around long?" The bartender uses a rag to wipe the puddles of beer from the bar surface and steps away, still within listening distance.

The barroom is uncomfortably quiet until Ben finally reaches for his serving of beer and Vic tosses several coins on the wooden bar top as payment. Everett peers down at the glass-handled mug and finally responds to Dutch, "Awhile."

The old rancher fiddles with the whiskey bottle before him and tips it toward Everett. "How about a drink?"

"Already got one."

The old rancher's keen eyes drift to Marlow, who is obviously listening, and back again to Everett. "Awhile, huh?" Dutch holds up his filled glass. "You fellas lookin' for a job?" He tips back his drink of whiskey and pours himself another. "I own most the land 'round here suitable for cattle. You ain't gonna try to rustle my stock or squat on my land, are you?"

The jaw muscles tighten along the side of Everett's shaven cheek at the mention of cattle rustling, but he remains outwardly calm and responds, "We'll take up here in town."

Dutch inquires of Everett curiously, "What for?"

"Have business to attend to."

"Yeah, that so?"

"Yep."

"There ain't much of any business to be had 'round these parts 'cept whiskey drumming and cattle ranching. What kinder business you propose to be in?"

Everett lifts his mug of beer and takes a long swallow. He flicks the clinging drips from his moustache with a swipe of a finger before responding in a low, steady tone to Dutch. "A good man was murdered on this day, at the edge of town." Everett tries to contain his swelling emotions as he continues, "His few cattle were stolen and a wagon burned."

Dutch gazes aside as he frowns and feigns concern. "Always sorry to find out about such happenings. I hear talk 'bout border Mexican bandits doin' that sort of thing of late." With a deliberate show of calm, Dutch tops off his whiskey. The rancher puts aside the bottle and cradles the tumbler. "What is it you call yourself and yer friends there?"

Everett raises his mug of beer to hold at chest level. "These two here are my brothers and official town deputies, Vic and Ben Colbert." Keeping his gaze set on Dutch to observe his reaction, Everett takes a swig of beer and firmly places the glass mug aside on the bar.

The rancher squints as he coughs uncomfortably and inquires, "Deputies, you say?"

Leaning to the side, Everett puts one elbow to the bar-top and lets his coat lapel fall open to reveal an official law-badge pinned on his vest. "My name is Everett, but you and your cowhands can jest refer to me as the town marshal." Dutch forces a somewhat cordial grin as Jenks, Curtis and the other cowboys look on dumbfounded. The silver-haired cattle rancher pushes his foreman aside, heaves his chest out and stands at his full height before the newly appointed lawman. "Ol' Polk ain't even cold on the slab, and now we got us three new law-dogs in town?"

The rancher downs another drink and takes his time pouring the last from the bottle. He glares at the lawmen. "You best be real careful to know your business 'round here." Dutch grumbles, "Jest 'cause some driftin' fella gets himself accidentally kilt don't justify an overabundance of law."

Everett clenches his jaw and spits his words at Dutch. "Shot, dragged… and lynched."

"How's that?" Dutch can't help but glance aside at Jenks and then to Curtis, who has moved out into the room.

Everett notices the skepticism in the old rancher's expression and takes a step nearer to Dutch. "When someone gets shot a dozen times, then dragged to the edge of town and strung up," Everett growls, "most folks wouldn't call that a case of accidental death."

Dutch narrows his gaze at Everett and nods slowly, understanding the situation more clearly. "No, I reckon not." The rancher raises the glass of whiskey and downs the last pour with a single gulp. Sneering slightly, Dutch slides the empty glass down the slab and steps away from the bar. "Marshal, ya best be careful. Out here, some border-livin' folk would just as soon shoot a meddling lawman as look at one." The rancher's eyes drop to the law-badge on Everett's vest. "That tin-star surely don't look big enough to hide behind." He scoffs and murmurs to his cowboys standing behind him, "Seems more of a target if yer askin' me." Dutch stumbles on the uneven plank floorboards as he steps away from the bar. He regains his composure and ushers Curtis along beside him. "Come on boy, let's git on home."

At the front entrance with a last glaring look at the three lawmen, Dutch marches out the saloon's double doors. Jenks watches the seasoned ranch boss exit with his son then takes up his position at the bar rail next to the other cowboys. He stares down at the remnants of his liquid refreshment and lifts his beer glass to take a drink. "Y'all are lawman now, eh? Best to watch out where you stick yer nose 'round these parts, else it could get pinched."

Pounding his beer mug on the bar with a loud thud, Vic steps forward and takes a position next to his brother. "Are you speaking to me, cowboy?"

Jenks glances over at Vic and gives a knowing smile. "Nope... Just having myself a thought." The ranch foreman finishes his drink and spins the empty glass mug on the wood bar top. He stands up straight, turns to move toward the exit and takes a brief evaluating look at the new set of lawmen. "We'll be seeing each other again soon, I expect."

Stepping past, Jenks stops at the doorway and glances back at the remaining *D/W* brand cowhands left in the saloon. His gaze stops at the back corner of the room before he steps out into the quiet night. Everett follows the foreman's fleeting glimpse and observes two familiar cowboys that he recognizes from the stagecoach encounter earlier, sitting at the back table. He lifts his glass mug of beer from the bar, takes a quick sip and strides toward them at the gaming table.

Chapter 9

The dimly lit saloon is mostly quiet with the exception of the shuffling snap from a deck of playing cards being dealt. Striding toward the game table at the rear of the room, Everett passes through occasional swaths of light created by oil lamps. He holds his mug of beer at chest level as he directs his attention to the familiar pair of cowboys seated at the table. "Where did you fellers go this afternoon?"

The two cowhands gaze up at the shiny tin star on Everett's chest as it reflects the light from the wall sconce. They nervously look to each other and then to the pair of men coming up behind, both pinned with deputy law-badges. "Sorry mister, we don't know what you're talking about." Everett scrutinizes the two cowboys until they uncomfortably bend their stares down to the cards on the table.

In a blurred flash of motion, Everett smashes his beer mug into the face of the closest cowhand and grabs the other by the crown of the hat, slamming his face into the tabletop. The beer-mug punched cowboy tumbles over to the floor as broken glass and wet foam drip from the empty chair seat. The other pinned cowboy tries to push back and squirms as the lawman gruffly presses the man's face into the card table. Everett leans in closer to inquire, "I asked you boys a question... Where you were this afternoon?"

Face-down on the table, the cowboy blows and snorts the cards away as his head is pressed harder to the surface. His eyes roll up to Everett, as he tries to pull back from him. "Mister, I don't know what the hell you're talking about!"

Everett looks to the other cowboy on the floor, splashed with spilt beer, holding his battered face. "How about you?"

The cowhand looks fearfully up at Everett through blood and beer-smeared features and shakes his head briskly. Vic and Ben stand back, not sure if they should help or hinder the acts of their enraged sibling. Everett lets the man up from the table, pushes him back in the chair and takes hold of the cowboy's neckerchief. He quickly twists the bandana like a tourniquet around the seated man's neck and continues his questioning. "I saw both of you at the stagecoach holdup... Were you there when they shot him?"

Only receiving a few choking gasps in response to the severe interrogation, Everett lifts the cowboy from his chair by the bib of his shirt and runs him back against the saloon wall. Ben glances at Vic, unsure, and the eldest brother bites his lip as he motions a sign for them to keep back for the time being. The cowboy on the floor remains collapsed in a clouded daze while his partner, held against the wall gapes, wide-eyed, at the punishing acts by the newly appointed lawman.

Not seeming to get any satisfying results, Everett jerks his revolver out and presses it hard into the man's abdomen. "Tell me who done the murdering deed or to hell with ya..." The cowboy's gasps turn to sobs as Everett cocks back the hammer and growls, "I'll gut shoot you right here and now." Vic finally takes a step forward and reaches out to calm his infuriated brother. "Everett, hold it now, we don't want that."

Ben comes around the other side of the table, ready to jump in and assist with the situation. "Easy now brother..."

Resuming the twisting choke-hold on the cowboy's neckerchief with the cocked handgun still pressed firm, Everett glances over with a half-crazed look on his features. "No Vic, I'm going to get some answers and settle this." Everett turns back and pushes the long barrel of the pistol harder into the man's ribcage. "I want the names of those who done the murderin' deed, and we're gonna get 'em!"

Covering his palm over the handle of his own holstered pistol, Ben gazes around the cleared-out room and notices the cowboy on the floor behind them start to draw his sidearm. He tries to step around his brother by the table and calls out. "Everett! Behind you! The floor..."

Everett whirls to see the bloody features of the cowboy on the plank floorboards, as he raises a cocked pistol at him. He retains his gripping hold on the cowboy against the wall as he instinctively swings his gun-hand around in self-defense. Not having time to think, Everett fires two consecutive shots. One bullet shatters a full whiskey bottle on the card table while the other gun-blast strikes its intended mark, hitting the *D/W* cowboy in the chest and sprawling him across the floor.

The room echoes in a deadly silence as the cloudy haze of black-powder smoke wafts through the air of the saloon. Still holding his grip of the other cowboy by the neck scarf, Everett turns back to face him. The unintended gunfire has quelled some of the fire from his belly, and he eases his choking hold on the man's throat. His mouth goes dry, but his voice remains firm as he growls at the quaking cowboy, "There will be some law and order in this damned town."

Everett takes a breath and glares with lethal intent. "You go tell them who done it... Best to turn themselves in." The lawman releases his twisted grip on the cowboy's neckerchief and steps back with the smoking pistol hanging loose at his side. "You go 'n tell them." He raises a pointed finger at the fear-struck cowboy and warns him, "Or heaven help me, I'll hunt each one of you down and kill y'all myself."

The cowboy against the wall coughs and rubs his tender, raw neck while nodding in agreement to the lawman. The recently discharged firearm still held at his side, Everett moves away and walks out through the front saloon doors. The deputized pair of brothers looks to the stunned cowboy, still situated against the wall, and then to the dead one face down on the floor in a puddle of beer, blood and broke glass. Bowing his head, Ben mutters. "We're in it now, brother."

Vic nods his head as he looks to the dark street outside. "Did you ever think we weren't?"

Chapter 10

The daytime interior of the marshal's office is cool and shady, with thick mud brick walls and wooden gun-port shutters. Everett leans back in a swivel chair across the desk from Vic, who plays a game of solitaire with a well-used deck of cards. The eldest brother slams the last remaining playing card down and wobbles his head. "Damn…"

Everett diverts his eyes from watching the empty street outside and turns to Vic. "Lose again?"

"Yup. Sure cain't seem to win with a partial deck. Seems ya need all the one-eyed royals to come out ahead."

There is a soft knock on the wood-beam doorframe at the open entry, and the standby doctor in town, Doc Watson, pokes his head in from the bright sunlight outside. "Hello?"

Vic gathers the cards before him together and stacks the deck to shuffle. "Come on in, Doc." The sheepish man enters cautiously and looks around the diffusely lit marshal's office.

Everett remains seated in his chair as the visitor stands silhouetted in the doorway. "Something we can do for you?"

Fidgeting with a button on his frock coat, Doc Watson gawps at Vic shuffling the deck of cards, then anxiously smoothes his hands down on his vest and turns to Everett. "Well fellas, I was a little hasty last night."

The desk chair squeaks as Everett readjusts and responds, "And how's that?"

"Well, ya see…"

Everett and Vic listen and wait patiently, as the doctor nervously paws the wood floor at the threshold of the office. Finally, he gets enough courage to look up at them and speak. "Ya see, I talked with the town committee, and they think we need to *elect* a new town marshal and not just appoint one."

There is a soft snap of worn playing cards as Vic shuffles the deck. "Y'all held one of these elections before?"

"Well, no… But we figure it might be best."

Everett thinks a moment, then nods and casually peels his coat back from covering the tin-star pinned on his vest. "Who is it that is on this town committee?"

The small town physician clearly doesn't want to be confrontational and keeps glancing out the doorway for any possible opportunity for escape. He straightens his coat front and replies, "Well, uh, hmm… You have to understand… Dutch Werner owns most of what you see around here."

Slapping the cards on the desk for another lineup of solitaire, Vic grunts, "So yer sayin' he *is* the town committee?"

The doctor takes a step back out of the office and nods. "You see, I was a little premature in appointing you to the town marshal job and your brothers as deputies, and I, uh… well, I need those badges back." Doc Watson stands visibly shaken in the doorway as he looks from the floor to Everett. "Would that be okay?"

Everett continues to recline back and relax in the tilted desk chair as he thinks a moment. He glances across the cards at Vic and then looks to the doctor in the entryway. "No."

The doctor stammers, "Wha… What?"

"If you want these badges returned, then you go and tell your committee they need to come take them from us." The doctor looks to Everett in shock as the newly appointed lawman continues. "You tell 'em to turn over the stolen cattle and the fellas that murdered the man outside of town, and we'll give up the office once they are properly dealt with."

Hesitant, the doctor looks outside to the empty street and then sputters, "You want me to tell them that?"

Everett affirms with a nod. "I was appointed with a job to do. I'm gonna follow it through till it's done."

The representative for the town looks down the vacant boardwalk and, tentatively, back into the marshal's office. "We're just a little concerned about people getting killed."

Vic pipes in as he moves up an ace of spades on his solitary game of cards. "Some folks have already been kilt."

Everett delivers a cold even stare toward Watson, as the doctor inches away from the doorway onto the boardwalk. "I'll take that concern into consideration." The doctor stands in the partial sun, midway across the porch, and nods his head with consent. "Okay then, I'll tell them that I took care of it."

Vic flips a card and places it along the lineup as he watches the doctor retreat across the street. He looks at Everett across from him and holds the remainder of the deck in hand. "These law badges really don't make a difference. We're all in now, whether we like it or not."

"Maybe so."

Vic is about to turn another card and pauses to reflect. He stares across the desktop at his younger brother and tries to make out his way of thinking. "You surely killed that feller last night and there's no going back from it."

Everett watches outside and then swivels his chair to look at Vic. "It didn't allow time to have a choice."

"No, it didn't. It was him or you. But we put ourselves in that situation." Everett nods in silence as Vic continues, "Just be clear... It's nearing on revenge that we're doing now, not justice. There's a line, and we're walkin' both sides of it."

"You and Ben can move on at any time."

Vic flips a card from the deck and pushes it aside. "We'll stick with ya brother, like always, 'til it's done."

The sounds of a lone horse pounding up the dirt street is heard approaching from inside. The galloping mount slides to a skidding stop in front of the marshal's office door and a billowing cloud of dust rolls in along the wooden floorboards. Vic leans forward and peers out a partially opened window. "Damn if that boy don't know how to lather up a horse."

The youngest Colbert brother walks through the open doorway and pats the fine layer of trail dirt from his clothing. The particles of dust hang in the beaming sun of the entry. Everett adjusts his chair toward the door, brings his feet down and questions his brother, "Find out anything?"

Ben removes his wide-brim hat and brushes his hand over the crown, unsuccessfully removing the top layer of dust. "A good bunch of Werner's beeves was stolen a week ago. Story goin' around is that it was a group of border Mexicans headed by a fellow named Hollister Tuckburrow."

Vic chimes in. "The feller that owns the saloon?"

"Yep, the one 'n the same."

Everett kicks a dusty boot over one knee and sits back in the creaky chair. "What else did ya find out?"

"A few folks are under the impression that it was this Tuckburrow and his Mexican bunch that rustled our cattle and murdered our uncle." Ben steps further inside the office and drags over a ladder-back chair. He swings it backwards and straddles the backrest to face the desk and his brothers. "Don't seem likely though, since they had a herd of stolen beeves with 'em already and were off selling 'em in Mexico 'bout the time we arrived."

Vic studies his solitaire layout, moves a card and peers up at Ben. "Werner's name come up?"

Along to Presidio

Ben brushes the thick film of dust from the top of his boots on the rear of his pants leg. "There's no question he's the big honcho around here. He's got a stranglehold on this burg, so no one says much about him."

The three brothers are quiet as they take in and contemplate the new information. Everett breaks the silence. "This Tuckburrow character, is he still in Mexico?"

Ben smiles. "He's supposed to be back any day now."

Vic thumbs at the corner of the cards and gazes at his young brother. "Would there be any hurry for him to return?"

Ben looks out the doorway across the street to the Barrelhouse. "I guess he has a saloon business to keep up..." Ben shrugs and adds, "Folks say he's got a woman he keeps."

Everett pushes up from his creaking chair and stands. He stares outside to the empty street of the border town and looks beyond the window shutter to the sweated horse at the hitching rail, with its head down, switching its tail at flies. "I'm going to do some trawling at Tuck's Barrelhouse." Everett adjusts his gun-belt and looks to the game of solitaire. "Vic, I want you to check more into that Werner outfit and see what they're really about. Find out if they're moving any new beeves around, or doing any branding out of season." Grabbing his hat from the row of wall pegs by the doorway, Everett adjusts his coat and covers over his holstered sidearm.

Ben stands from the chair and hikes up his gun-belt. "Expect to mix it up a bit, brother?" Ben half-grins as he taps the butt of his pistol. "Want me to go with you or hang here?" He swings the chair away and looks outside.

Everett puts his hat on and walks out to the porch. "That horse of yours is played out. Take mine and ride with Vic." He steps from the boardwalk into the bright sunshine. "We'll see what comes of it." With a determined stride, he marches across the street toward Tuck's Barrelhouse.

Chapter 11

Despite being the only drinking establishment in town, the daytime interior of the Barrelhouse is not a boon of activity. Two men play cards at a table, and Marlow, the bartender, stands behind the bar with a knee hiked up to lean on as he stares out the front windows. A hint of wonder crosses his features when he sees Everett cross the street, advance up the steps and walk inside. "Good day to ya, Marshal."

Everett nods as he approaches the bartender, and his narrowed gaze quickly scans the entire room of occupants. Marlow grins perceptively, as he meets him midway down the polished wood slab. He tilts his head and catches a glimpse of the partially concealed law badge under Everett's coat lapel. "You still the law in town?"

"So far."

"What'll you have?"

"I'll take a mug."

Marlow turns and reaches for a glass-handled vessel. "Nothing a touch stronger, perhaps? With the color of talk 'round here, thought you might be needin' it."

"What sort of talk is that?" Everett puts a hand to the bar as Marlow turns to fill the glass mug from the beer keg.

The bartender glances over his shoulder at the lawman. "Oh, just some off-the-cuff comments about you and your brethren getting booted out of town... or worse."

Everett peers around and shrugs, "That it?"

"Ain't that enough?"

"Who's gonna do it?"

The mug of beer fills to the top and the layer of covering foam spills over the rim and drips down. "Can't say, but they'll make themselves known soon 'nough, I'm sure." Marlow swipes the top of the mug with a paddle knife and cuts the foam. "Personally, I like it when the pot gets stirred. It becomes more interesting 'round here when folks are riled."

A shadow passes before the windows and a womanly figure fills the doorway. Everett, Marlow and the few others turn to the entrance and watch her come in through the double, entryway doors. Dressed in dated, but elegant, feminine attire, the woman has a distinct saunter to her walk. Charlotte Torres makes her grand arrival and leans her ample bosom onto the rail of the bar top. A fair-skinned fiery redhead, Charlotte's eyes gleam with the experience of her years along with an indifference to her age-old occupation.

Marlow sets the filled mug of beer in front of Everett and reaches for a special reserve bottle from beneath the bar. He takes the jug, with its swirling contents, and a petite silver tumbler to the waiting woman perched at the end of the slab. In soft breaths and whispers to the bartender, the name Tuck can be heard with Polk and reference to the new marshal.

Turning slightly from the bar, Everett attempts to listen in on the pair's private conversation while giving the false impression of observing the trivial game of cards at the table. He lifts the mug of beer from the bar top and takes a short sip. The two gamblers at the gaming table glance over at Everett, as he leans an elbow to the bar, and his coat lapel falls away to reveal the star-badge. The lawman lifts his mug in a friendly gesture to the card players and grins. "Don't mind me boys. Jest appeciatin' a good game."

Everett notices behind, as Marlow exits to a back room. Charlotte makes inquisitive eyes at the lawman leaned on the bar rail and slides her hand down the polished surface to him. From the corner of his eye, Everett notices her moving closer but pretends to keeps his attention focused on the game table.

The woman in the fancy, sporting dress stops beside Everett and waits for him to notice her. She pours a drink from her bottle and places it back on the bar top with a thud. Everett glances behind, offers a casual nod, then turns back to observing the card game. Impatient to attract his attention, Charlotte places her hand on his shoulder and moves it along to the front of his lapel. "What is your name, Señor?"

Surprised by her local accent, Everett glances back and speaks aside to her. "Same as was mentioned over yonder." The woman is taken aback slightly, but her hand remains on his coat. Everett tilts his head to the other end of the room where she had the recent conversation with the bartender. "What's your name, Miss?"

"Charlotte Torres."

"And what do you do, Miss Torres?"

"I am help to Señor Tuck when he plays." The woman resumes caressing her hand over the shoulder of Everett's coat and slides her probing fingers along his vest in a familiar way. He looks down at her hand and takes hold of it at the wrist. "So, when does this infamous Señor Tuck get back to town from his business trip?" He gives her slender wrist a firm squeeze and she lets out a tiny yelp.

The players at the table glance over momentarily and then elect to mind their own affairs and continue their game. Not getting any sort of answer, Everett twists her arm slightly. Charlotte responds by hissing at him, "He is my man, and he comes and goes as he pleases."

Everett studies her makeup-enhanced features and her wild, red-hair, then eases his grip before speaking quietly. "How does it happen that a fair-skin, natural ginger speaks with a Mexican accent and is named like a French whore?"

Her pupils go dark and dance with anger, as she narrows her eyes to slits and glares daggers at the lawman. "Me father was Irish and mi madre was a full-blood Mezkin" Charlotte smirks as she glances to the badge on Everett's vest. "We are all whores at some time in our lives, are we not?"

"How do you mean?"

"Any man hiding behind a tin-star is merely a whore for the one in town who has the most money to pay for it."

"And who might that be?"

"I cannot say, but everybody knows..."

Charlotte stifles a squeal as Everett twists her arm a touch, and she squirms. The card game pauses again as the two men hold their play and look to the pair at the bar. Everett puts on a façade with his friendliest demeanor and nods to the men at the table. "Excuse us, gentlemen."

Dragging Charlotte along behind, Everett moves down the bar toward the double front doors. She tries to wriggle and twist free from his firm grip, but he holds her wrist tightly. Charlotte doesn't hold back any as she curses her restrainer. "Unhand me Señor! You dirty, murdering swine with your phony tin-star that means nothing to me. Let me go!"

Continuing out through the wide-open front doors, Everett drags her outside to the covered porch of the saloon. He ushers her along the front boardwalk and escorts Charlotte around to the side of the building, away from the main street. A few steps into the alleyway, he stops and swings her around to face him. "I would like that tin-star, which you removed from my vest and care nothing about, returned to me."

Charlotte stares up at Everett and then darts away, attempting to flee, but he pulls her back. She hisses at him, "Let me go, I took nothing."

She tries to twist away but Everett yanks her close and clenches her in a tight embrace. Their faces move extremely close, as if they were about to kiss and Everett speaks low. "Do I have to search you for it?"

With no viable alternative, Charlotte stops struggling and stares up into the clear eyes of the mustached lawman. She tosses her red hair back from her bare shoulders defiantly and reaches around his holding grip to the side of her blouse. The lawman relaxes his hug as she feels around a moment and comes out with the pilfered tin-star.

He pushes back from her a step and stares coolly. Charlotte offers an innocent smirk and seductively slides the marshal badge into his accessible vest pocket. Her thieving fingers caress his shirt front and she taps his chest kindly. "What are you going to do? Shoot me like that cowboy?"

Everett accepts the insult with the obvious reference. "No, but you should be taught a lesson."

"What can you possibly do to me? Put me in your jail? You must know, I am Tuck's and you cannot keep me."

Everett retains his embrace on her and pulls her closer. He breathes easy and slowly leans down toward her face. "That really depends on when this Tuck gets back in town." Inviting him, she pushes up on her toes and puts her chin up, expecting a kiss. Everett stares into her alluring eyes and turns his cheek to her, peering down the alley to the street. "As loyal as the day is long, I see."

Feeling the intended slight of his blunt rejection, Charlotte attempts to pull her arms away from Everett's grasp and curses him in fluent Spanish. *"You are nothing to me, and can kiss my brother's black cat's ass!"*

Everett twirls her around and splays her, face down, over an empty barrel at the front corner of the saloon building. He hitches up the top layers of her skirting to uncover her bare backside and braces her there. Conflicted, her eyes flutter behind at him expectantly and he hauls off and inflicts a hard slap across her exposed rump.

Aghast, her features fill with horrified shock as his palm pulls back and spanks her again with a solid smack. Charlotte kicks out her legs and screeches like a wildcat, "Tuck will kill you for this! He will be back tonight and he will kill you, I say!" Everett reels his hand back for another swing and cracks it hard across her buttocks again.

Charlotte glimpses out to the main street and squawks back at Everett positioned behind her. "You'll pay, Señor! When the stagecoach arrives, you'll answer to Tuckburrow!" Everett inflicts one last, hard spank to her exposed backside and relinquishes his dominance. Cursing under her breath, she quickly rights herself, spins around to glare at him and touches her tender bottom.

Everett stares at Charlotte, as he takes the law badge from his pocket and deliberately pins it to his vest again. "You'll need to be watchin' that filthy mouth of yours too." Everett glances to the murky water settled in the horse trough, "In either language, or I'll wash it out for you the next time." She spits aside and murmurs a curse under her breath. Everett shakes his head and brushes the metal star on his vest with his coat sleeve. "You're also a damn poor thief."

Charlotte suddenly lashes out and smacks Everett open-handed across the jaw. "I am very good at what I do!" Hurriedly, she grabs up her layered skirting and scurries away from arm's reach before he can retaliate. Gingerly touching his reddened cheek, Everett stands and watches her.

Along to Presidio

As she flees around the front corner of the Barrelhouse, he steps from the side alley and back up to the front walkway. His cheek still stinging, the lawman glances around and lets his gaze linger on a high window with a view of the street. Behind the wavy glass pane, a curtain flutters and Everett takes note of an observing presence.

Chapter 12

Everett stands at the double entry to Tuck's Barrelhouse positioned with his outlined form darkened at the threshold. He strides inside with the hollow thump of spur-heeled boots on the wood-plank floor and returns to his position at the bar. The saloon's interior is quiet, as Everett glances to the rear barroom table where a fresh stain darkens the wood floorboards from the night prior. The card-playing men at the table gawk inquisitively at him, and he offers a friendly nod. "You may continue your game, gentlemen."

Uncertain of the new lawman in town, the two slowly return to their intermittent card game and leave him to his task of standing at the bar. Everett takes up his beer mug and swallows down the remaining contents, as Marlow comes from the back room. He walks over to Everett's empty glass. "Another drink for you, Marshal?"

"Nope." The low sound of ticking catches Everett's attention, and he studies the decorative hands on the large-faced clock perched behind the bar. "That timepiece regular?"

"Yep. All the way from St. Louis."

Everett removes a pocket watch from his vest and compares the clock hands. "What time is the stage line due?"

"Well, that is something that ain't particularly regular. It kin be hard for folks to get in or out of a small town." Marlow lowers his voice a bit and speaks under his breath. "Should be here within the hour, maybe two if it happens today at all and they ain't had problems."

"What sort of problems?"

"Aw, anything can happen. Wheels fall off, horses get bungled up or the driver is in his cups…"

"Road bandits?"

"Ain't had problems with them, but could happen."

The lawman offers an acquiescent nod, looks in the empty beer mug and pushes it aside. Everett tucks his whiskered lip to his lower and swipes his finger across his mouth and moustache to wipe any clinging dribbles of foam. He gestures goodbye to the card-players at the table and turns to walk toward the front doors, as Marlow calls after him, "Safe travels Marshal. Or, will we be seein' you again?"

Everett continues through the doorway and replies over his shoulder. "Could be… I sure ain't leavin' town." Marlow turns to glance at the clock behind the bar and then back at the sunlit entryway, as Everett steps off the porch and descends into the empty street. The lawman pauses to look around before strolling toward the livery and coach depot.

~*~

Two horseback riders lope their mounts to the top of a small hill and look out over an expansive spread of ranchland. The two Colbert brothers sit their mounts and observe a vast herd of grazing cattle congregating at a muddy watering hole. Ben turns aside to his brother Vic and whistles low and quiet. "If our little herd is mixed up with these beeves, it would take a month of Sundays to pick 'em out."

Vic contemplates the extensive gathering of cowhide. "Yeah, if they have any smarts though, they'll keep our stock separate 'til they git a chance to put 'em past a runnin' iron 'n alter the brands."

"They're prob'ly doing that somewhere right now."

Vic nods in agreement and leans on the saddle horn. "Won't be too far 'cause they'll want to turn 'em into the mix as soon as the work is done." The older brother glances up at the afternoon sun to gauge the time and gathers up his reins. "Let's head back to town." His eyes travel over the sprawling landscape that rolls along to small mountains in the distance. "There's nothing more can be done at present. We'll talk with Everett and start again on the morrow."

Ben casts a final gaze across the foraging herd and the unsettled territory. He watches Vic urge his horse to a trot in the direction of town and turns his horse to follow after him. While the two riders travel away, the dip in the terrain around the watering hole disappears into the landscape, obscuring the sight and sound of grazing cattle.

~*~

The sun begins to set low in the western sky and Everett sits, leaned back on two legs of a slatted chair outside the livery barn. He leisurely draws on a cigar and watches the grey, smoky exhale dissipate into the evening glow of the sky. A motion in the distance and a faint sound on the breeze catches his attention, and he lets the chair drop to all fours.

The rumbling cadence of hoof-falls from a team-hitched stagecoach can be heard approaching the far reaches of town. As the passenger coach comes clearly into sight, a trailing cloud of dust rises and lingers. After a short time the four-up team of horses pulls the coach through the middle of town and clamors to a halt in front of the livery stables and depot. The stagecoach driver peers down at Everett and takes a moment to recognize him.

The lawman nods and puts a finger to his wide hat brim as salutation to the driver. "Evenin', Sir."

Everett stands back a few paces, as the driver tosses two sets of luggage from the top roof rack to the dusty street. The driver stares at Everett inquisitively a while before using the front wheel spokes to climb down from his high perch. "We cross paths again, eh? Nice law badge yer sportin'."

Stepping nearer to the driver at the front wheel axle, Everett peers into the dark interior of the passenger coach. "How many folks you got aboard this trip?" The driver moves closer to the town marshal and nudges Everett with his elbow. "Eh feller, where's ol' Polk?" Attempting to identify the shadowed features of the two passengers inside the coach, Everett turns to address the driver. "Had a health problem."

"That arm of his actin' up?"

"Yep, killed him."

The stagecoach driver ponders the morbid thought and then huffs and shrugs, as he grabs up the luggage from the street to move from blocking the descent from the stagecoach. "Hell, he never helped with the baggage or loading neither." The driver sets the personal belongings across the way and returns to unlatch the coach door. With a twist of the handle, the hinged panel door swings wide and Everett waits to observe the occupants inside.

A stout man in formal clothing, with a cane in hand, appears at the coach door. He gazes around the seemingly unoccupied border town with bulging, glazed-over, opium-soaked pupils and smiles inquisitorially at the town marshal. In a posh theatrical drawl, the stocky man speaks out as if addressing a full audience from center stage, "Hello fine sir, and a pleasant day to you." He raises the handle of his cane and continues his introduction. "I am Jasper Montgomery Lucas the III and hail from the Big Windy Theatre in Chicago. I am charged with the performance of three Shakespearian tragedies and other assorted monologues at the local stage under the peculiar moniker of Tuck's Barrelhouse. Could you, sir, please point me in that general direction?"

Everett takes a moment to digest the melodramatic ramblings and points a finger to the rear of the stagecoach. "The Barrelhouse is due west."

J.M. Lucas steps down from the stagecoach, looks around at the desolate town with its ramshackle buildings and does a slight tip of his narrow-brimmed hat. "Would you be so kind as to have my bags sent to the hotel?" In a slow fluid motion, the actor pivots on a heel and ambles in the direction of the Barrelhouse

Everett observes the intoxicated performer's departure, then turns his attention back to the interior of the stagecoach. Appearing in the coach doorway, a figure with a slim frame and uncut beard emerges to eye the lawman suspiciously. Outfitted in a faded coat and an assembly of worn clothing, the mysterious gent offers a contrived smile toward Everett as he lowers himself from the stagecoach. "That there fellow has a strange wind about 'im. The only times he could be understood clear was when he was pulling the cork to that damned opiate bottle." The stagecoach passenger steps down and plants his dusty boots in the street. "Should turn out to be an interestin' performance."

Everett observes as the man adjusts his coat and vest. "Would you happen to be Hollister Tuckburrow?"

The scraggly gentleman smoothes out a coat sleeve and dusts a shoulder before glimpsing the badge on Everett's vest. "Well, Mister Lawman, just call me Tuck."

"Okay, Tuck."

Tuck scratches his long chin-whiskers and muses. "Whereabouts is Marshal Polk?"

"He's passed on."

"Ya mean dead?"

"Yep."

"You kill 'im?"

"Nope."

"How'd you get the job?"

"Duly appointed."

Tuck walks over to take up his leather duffle and turns to look at Everett curiously. "Dutch Werner hire you?"

"No."

A mischievous glimmer flickers in Tucks eyes as he tilts his head. "Then you ain't really got the job now, do ya?"

Everett sweeps his coat aside to reveal the entire badge along with the firearm at his hip. "We need to talk some."

"I need a drink."

"That'd be fine."

Tuck nods agreeably and gestures Everett toward the barrelhouse saloon. "In that case, my drinking establishment is at your service." Everett affirms his acceptance of the invitation and the men move in step beside another as they stride down the dry, dusty main thoroughfare. Behind them, the stagecoach driver retires the hitched team, leaving the stagecoach abandoned in front of the livery.

Chapter 13

Late in the afternoon, the glowing orange orb of sun dips to the horizon and casts long shadows across the desolate town. Tuck quickens his step to move ahead of Everett and climbs the stairs at the front porch of the saloon. He peers through the windows at the few occupants inside and puts his booted foot to the double entry and pushes it clear. The doors slam open and rattle back on their hinges as Tuck strides into the saloon, slaps his hand on the bar top and hollers, "Wahoooy! I'm back from the deserts of Sonora and have a mighty thirst. Marlow, set us up with some refreshment."

Crossing a narrow shaft of sunlight streaming in from the last remnants of day, Everett follows Tuck into the bar. The slight-framed saloon-owner hoists his leather satchel to the bar-top and turns to scan the few occupants of the room. Tuck scratches his neck under his whiskers and then peers at Everett as they wait for drinks. "So, ol' Polk has expired. How'd it happen?"

Marlow pours a glass full of whiskey, slides the drink to Tuck and then pours the same for Everett. He leaves the bottle between them and moves a few steps away to an easy, listening distance. Everett gingerly raises the tumbler to take a short sip from the generous pour and eyes Tuck over the rim. "Most thought it was a feller by the name of Melvin Walper who shot 'im, but it turns out he just died."

Tuck raises his whiskey glass in the fading daylight and pours the amber liquid down his throat. Paused with his hand gripping the bar rail, the saloon keeper closes his eyes. He takes a sudden breath, slaps his hands and fills another. "Walper, huh? He's one of Werner's hands."

"Dutch Werner?"

Tuck smiles. "Yeah... Met him yet?"

Everett places his beverage on the bar and rotates the whiskey glass with his fingers. "We've met."

Tuck grins, takes a swallow from his fresh pour and sets down the remainder. He leans back on the rail and gazes out to the open room. "How'd you come to take on that star?"

"Got some business to tend to."

Tuck studies the lawman and smirks from beneath his whiskers. "Got some revenge business of sorts to handle?"

Everett brings up his drink of whiskey and finishes it. "I have a few things to settle."

The saloon keeper looks around at the occupants, of the mostly empty barroom, and out the front doors to the street. "Ain't much opportunity for any other business in town... None worth sticking around for, anyways." Tuck grabs the bottle to uncork it and reaches over to pour Everett another. "So, you ain't leaving this burg till it's done or you're done?"

"Seems that way."

Tuck gazes past Everett's shoulder to see the figures of two unknown men cross the street and enter the doorway. Distracted, he watches curiously as the pair step into the saloon and take a seat at the table directly behind Everett. "Marshal, I wish you luck with your endeavor in retribution, but I hope to have us an understanding."

Tuck's eyes drift to the two unfamiliar men at the table as Everett responds, "How's that?"

Along to Presidio

Tuck takes another guzzling swig from his whiskey drink while keeping his eyes on the newcomers seated at the table. He makes a subtle motion to Marlow and the bartender returns the directed gesture with a nod. Tuck holds his glass tumbler at chest level and speaks to Everett in a low tone. "Despite a few troubles, I've got a pretty good situation 'round here that I don't need meddled with."

Behind the bar, Marlow reaches under the counter past a cut-barreled shotgun to grab a small caliber pocket revolver. He dutifully inspects the hideaway gun and slips it in the back waistband of his pants. Keenly aware, Everett glimpses the bartender's concealed movement but keeps his focus on Tuck. "And what situation is that?"

The whiskered, saloon owner raises his glass of whiskey in a salutation to the marshal and takes a swallow. "Let's jest say, I won't interfere with your sort of illicit business if you don't mind mine."

The bartender, with the handle of the revolver poking out from the back waist of his trousers, moves around from behind the bar into the room. Tuck pours another as Marlow approaches the two customers with a cleaning towel in hand to wipe the dust from the table. Everett puts his attention on Tuck's fresh pour of whiskey and replies, "Seems fair... Unless your business becomes mine."

The saloon owner makes note of the lawman's obvious disregard of the seemingly unacquainted men seated behind. Taking up the bottle by the neck, he eyes Everett cautiously. "With that sort of mule-headed attitude, it's a wonder you met Dutch and he didn't kill you already."

Everett taps his finger on the bar and stares ahead. "Could be, he thought you were the right man for that job."

Tuck offers a grin beneath his lip-whiskers and leans over to Everett. "You might have something there, Marshal."

The lawman watches as the saloon owner pulls back his overcoat to cover his open palm over his holstered sidearm. Everett glances over to the men seated at the table as they watch the confrontation. "This ain't the time or place for it."

Tuck follows Everett's gaze and makes eyes with Marlow on standby. "There is no time like the present."

There is a slight scuffing of chair legs and Everett tilts his head toward the gentlemen at the table with their coats pulled back to reveal deputy badges and hands on pistols. Tuck forces a gentle smile as he looks past Everett's shoulder, but keeps his palm covering the handle of his holstered gun. He stares at Marlow nearby and returns his attentive gaze to the lawman. "I see you fellers already know each other?"

"Born 'n bred of the same stock."

Tuck takes a moment to assess the circumstances of the badge-wearing associates versus Marlow with the hideaway. He takes after another quick glimpse around the room before giving a blatant shake of his head to the tentative bartender. The saloon owner peacefully ends the confrontation with the lawman before him, as he puts both hands to the edge of the bar-top and lets his coat cover over his holstered firearm. "Should've figured it as such when I saw them fresh faces 'round here. I'll have to keep a careful eye on you, Marshal."

"I'll be sure to do the same."

There is a slight shuffle of commotion at the front entryway when Jasper Montgomery Lucas the III swings open the doors to make his appearance. "Hello, gentlemen and... My, oh my... Where might I ask, are all the working ladies?" The intoxicated actor enters the saloon while stumbling over his words. "I am J. M. Lucas the Third of... Oh, whatever. Who would be the first that would like to buy me a drink?"

Everyone's attention is diverted from the boisterous actor as one of the card-players in the room lets out a howl, "You damn, black-hearted cheat! I saw that!"

The card player seated across the table pulls his revolver, draws the hammer back as the barrel rises above the table and lets the gun bark with a flaming flash of powder. The poorly-aimed bullet tears into the wall directly ahead, as the other player draws his own firearm and returns the shot. Before the deafening echo of the exchanged gun blasts fade, all occupants of the saloon have dashed for cover.

Everett and Tuck crouch down beside each other near the end of the bar to avoid the careless discharge of firearms. Several more gunshots ring out as the quarrelsome duo continues to heatedly curse at one another. Tuck peeks out from cover at the gun-fighting card-players and ducks back. "Hey Marshal, ain't it your job to do something?"

Everett holds his hand up to silence the saloon owner. "*Shush*, I'm counting their shots."

Tuck looks at him peculiarly then peeks around the side of the bar into the saloon again. Several more rounds are fired and Tuck pulls back to safety. "They've hit everything else in the bar 'xcept one another."

Everett holds his fingertips as he listens and counts. There is a deadly silence as the clicking of spent cylinders echoes in the smoke-filled room. Tuck shakes his head and glances down at Everett's hand. "They finally empty yet?"

Everett stands and moves around the bar to call out at the men at odds standing opposite the upturned game table. "Come now fellas, that's 'nough." The lawman moves toward the two gunmen as they continue to circle the table with pistol barrels still smoking. Still worked up in a tizzy, one card-player raises his gun and clicks it on an empty chamber. Everett reaches out and grabs away the pistol from his hand. "I said, that's 'nough!"

Everett takes the card-playing, wannabe gunfighter by the vest collar and shoves him toward the front entry doors. "The both of you, get out of here!" Everett motions with the barrel of the apprehended pistol at the other card-player to holster his firearm. He gestures toward the double doorway. "Git yerself home or spend the night in a jail cell."

The accused card cheat looks down innocently at his empty handgun and graciously returns it to his hip holster. He receives an approving nod from the town marshal and scoots toward the front doors after the other guilty culprit. Everett scans around the barroom, as Vic and Ben stand up from their hiding place at the table.

Noticing the quarrelsome pair ready to start the fight up again by the doorway, Everett waves his brothers over. "Get them wags outside and along on their separate ways." Vic steps around the table and grabs one of the men by the shoulder of the vest while Ben takes the other by the elbow. They escort the offending card-players out to the boardwalk and split ways to opposite ends of town.

Tuck stands and moves out to the center of the room. He observes through the front panels of windows as Vic and Ben cross paths in the street with their charges heading in opposite directions. Everett tosses the empty pistol to the bar-top with a heavy thud and peers around the quiet, smoke-hazed barroom. "Anyone hurt?"

There is a general murmur of reprieve as the few remaining occupants in the saloon pick themselves up from the floor. The sound of scooting chairs and clanking glass returns to the room as everyone settles in to drinking again. Someone calls out from the crowd at the saloon entrance. "They shot the actor!"

Along to Presidio

In the front corner of the saloon, the actor, J.M. Lucas is slumped on the floor unmoving. Striding across the room, Tuck squats down next to the rumpled body of the performer as Everett walks over to investigate. He stands over Tuck while the saloon owner examines the limp body.

"Well, Tuckburrow… He shot?"

Tuck shakes his head and gives the red-faced actor a slap across his drool glistened jaw. "He's passed out cold." The saloon owner wipes the drunken slobber from his hand on the actor's coat and, with a snort of obvious disgust, stands up beside Everett. "If his soured breath doesn't kill anyone, you'll have an occasion without casualties." Tuck turns to look at the bartender across the room and waves him over. "Marlow, get someone to take him over to the hotel."

Everett follows Tuck back to the bar, and they watch as Marlow and two others try to get the slouching mass of the inebriated actor out the wide doorway. Tuck shakes his head and pours himself another drink. "Some investment he was."

Everett pushes his glass aside, declining the offer of another drink. "Who's the poor grudger that pays his wage?"

"I am."

"Oh. Hmm."

Tuck takes a swallow of whiskey and rakes his fingers down through his beard. "Found him down in Mexico. Should've known he was done for good when he didn't sober much in two days of travel." The saloon owner takes another drink and grabs up the whiskey bottle for yet another refill.

Everett turns to the open doorway and looks to the dark buildings in the street beyond. "I'd best be on my way."

Tuck pours the last of the whiskey from the bottle into his glass and rolls the empty container down the long bar-top. A smile appears beneath his bush of whiskers as he speaks, "Glad to make your acquaintance, Marshal."

Everett looks at Tuck and nods in reply. "Likewise."

Tuck leans against the bar rail and holds his glass up. "Come on by here tomorrow evening 'n see that fellow perform... if he's able."

Everett gives the bar a tapping thump with his fingertips and turns to leave. "I'll do that." As the lawman steps outside to the street and disappears into the dusky night, Tuck reaches over the bar and grabs himself another bottle.

Chapter 14

The expanse of street fronting the marshal's office is deserted except for three saddled horses in the partial shade of the overhanging porch roof. They munch at clumps of dry grass around the hitching rail post and swish their tails at an occasional fly in the warming sun. A wooden door slams somewhere in town, and the street settles to an empty silence.

Inside the cool interior of the marshal's office, Everett and Vic sit on opposite sides of the desk while the older brother shuffles through the deck of incomplete playing cards. Ben stands at the gun-port window shutters and stares out at the desolate town street. He paces the floor in the early light of day and keeps a lookout for any sort of movement in town. Everett rocks back in the squeaky desk chair, softly whistling part of a tune as Vic puts his elbows to the desk and carefully lays out a game of cards. "Ya know Vic, that stack of one-eyed royals ain't improved any since the last time you played."

Vic nods and flips another card. "Yep, 'n I expect the same damn results on account of it." Ben stops at the window, peers out the gun-port opening and glimpses a momentary flash of motion behind the livery barn at the end of the street. He glances at his brothers then moves to the upright rifle rack. "Looks to be, Tuck is on his way out of town somewheres." Ben removes one of the rifles from the gun rack and levers the action. "He slipped out the back of the livery, heading south."

Everett sits the creaky chair forward, pushing it back to stand, and Vic smacks the partial deck of cards on the desk. The older brother swipes his hand across the playing cards to gather them up. Everett smirks across the desk at the pile. "Don't ya want to finish out yer game?"

"Already know how it'll end." Vic puts on his hat and steps to the door, as Ben tosses him a long gun from the rack. Ben takes another rifle down and supports it under his arm. He waits for Everett to put on his coat and follows outside to the waiting horses. Standing on the boardwalk, the brothers gaze to the edge of town at the trail of dust moving away.

~*~

Mounted horseback, Tuck rides along the rocky landscape of the southwestern border region at an easy, unhurried trot. He smoothes down his moustache and beard as his medium length hair blows back with the breeze below the narrow brim of his felt hat. Only once does he look behind, scanning the surrounding terrain before continuing on.

At a considered distance behind, the three horseback brothers follow the set of hoof tracks on the ground and the telltale dust rising from the single rider moving ahead. Keeping to the cover of the scrub trees and dipping terrain, they hold up and wait while the rider crests a small ridge. They peer aside at each other as the trailed rider drops down and disappears into a ravine.

The lone horseman travels down a steep path into a secluded gorge and reins up in front of a rustic adobe shack. The stagnant air hangs heavy and the horse snorts uneasy. With a suspicious gaze skyward, Tuck eyes the far hilltops, dismounts and goes inside.

~*~

In the secluded valley, the remote shack sits idly quiet. The lone horse stands tied alongside the mud-brick building. A small bird flits between branches on scrub bushes and a momentary breeze flaps the blanket covering in the window. The low muffled tone of a voice is heard from inside, and the dark outline of a lone person appears in the shaded entryway. Suddenly, a volley of popping gunshots explodes from the surrounding cover of brush.

The gut-shot figure in the doorway tumbles away from the blanketed cabin entrance to reveal Hollister Tuckburrow standing alone and then quickly diving back inside for cover. Obscured in the shadows of the interior, Tuck draws his pistol and fires a return shot toward the unexpected bushwhackers. Several volleys of gunfire hail down from the adjacent hillside towards the isolated mud-brick abode.

~*~

A good distance away from the crested ridge, Everett exchanges a quick glance with his brothers, as the distinctive sounds of gunshots pop and echo from down in the valley. The three simultaneously unsheathe their rifles from leather saddle-scabbards and spur their horses on down the trail. Stopping just short of the ridge above the encircled attack on the adobe dwelling, the three brothers quickly dismount and tie-off their horses to low branches. They proceed down into the ravine on foot with rifles tucked tight to their shoulders.

~*~

Splaying chunks of straw and dried-mud splinter off the brick building, as hot lead splatters into the adobe walls. Tuck extends his pistol out the front door and hammers off several gunshots to locations where the burnt-powder haze lingers over low-lying scrub. He pulls back inside to reload during a brief respite when the barrage of shooting subsides. Tuck cautiously pokes his head out to the edge of the door opening and hollers, "What'd you come to git?"

Several more rounds of popping gunshots erupt from the hillside undergrowth, followed by a disconcerting silence. In the dim interior of the shack, Tuck creeps along the sunk dirt floor and eases up to a critter hole in the crumbling wall. He peeks outside to see Melvin Walper and several range-outfitted cowboys jockeying for different shooting positions. He pokes the tip of his pistol barrel through the small hole, takes careful aim and squeezes the trigger.

A telltale puff of gunpowder smoke comes from low on the adobe wall of the assaulted dwelling. The cowboys duck down and Melvin Walper catches the pistol shot in the upper chest, dropping his rifle as he spins to the dirt with a grunt. The fierce volley of ambushing gunfire explodes once again, as Tuck stays low on the floor to avoid the torrent of hot lead bouncing through the blanketed doorway and windows.

Just as quickly as everything started, the shooting of guns comes to an abrupt end, and an eerie stillness envelops the smoke-clogged valley. Only a slight hint of movement can be seen through the dense obstruction of concealing scrub. The grey cloud of expended black-powder hangs thick in the air and drifts around the adobe shack.

Waiting for a moment after the hiatus in the attack, Tuck crawls on his belly across the floor to peek out the door. Mostly all is quiet with the exception of a wounded cowboy whimpering dying breaths in the bushes of the near hillside. Tuck listens to the almost tranquil surroundings and calls out, "Hallo! Do y'all surrender?"

The Colbert brothers step out from the scrub, cocking recently-fired long guns that still smoke and are at the ready. Ben and Vic hold their rifles and scan their aim toward the hillside as the middle brother approaches the adobe shack. Everett looks to the blanket covered doorway and speaks out, "Tuckburrow, you still in there?"

Inside the bullet-riddled shack, Tuck gets up from the floor and dusts off his shirt front. "Yep! Still alive yet too."

Everett stops at the threshold, peers into the dank interior, but remains outside. Leaned on the mud-brick wall he calls out to Tuck, "How many are inside with you?"

"Jest me is all."

Everett keeps his back to the wall and scans the ridge. He steadies his gaze out to the scrubby cover of the ambush and his eyes lower to the curled body just outside the door. "How many were out here?"

Tuck stands, half-shadowed inside the dwelling, and reloads the spent chambers on his six-gun. "One or two less of them bushwhackers now, I figure."

Everett glances at Tuck, still hiding in the shack, and waves him outside. "You can come on out, they're gone."

Tuck pushes the blanket aside from the door opening, stands in the mid-afternoon light and peers around curiously. He nudges the body on the ground by the entrance to find him unresponsive. "Nice of you fellas to jest happen along."

"Who's that with ya?"

"You could ask 'im, Marshal, but he's dead."

"That's why I'm askin' you."

Everett looks up from the ambush-killed man, and Tuck shrugs innocent, "Don't know. Suppose he lived here?"
Annoyed at Tuck's obvious put-on at aloofness, Everett responds, "Why the bushwhacking?"

Tuck takes a breath and looks to Everett suspiciously. "Depends on who was doin' the shootin'."

Ben stands a short distance from the cabin and waves Everett over to where he found something in the lower scrub. Tuck follows along behind the lawman, and they both stare down at the mortally-wounded cowboy laid out in the dirt. "Well, Marshal, that's yer ol' pal, Melvin Walper."

"Suppose he's here on Dutch Werner business?"

Tuck shrugs and kicks a booted toe at the body as it takes its last dying breath. "He ain't talking now, either."

Vic joins them and peers down at the deceased cowboy. He looks at Tuck and then turns to Everett with a grunt, "There's another one of them ambushing fellas over there."

Everett turns to where Vic gestures. "Dead?"

"Finally."

The badge-wearing trio of brothers stands with Tuck near the adobe shack and the lifeless body on the ground. Everett turns to Tuck. "What are you doing here?"

"Mindin' my own business, how about you?"

Everett glances over at his brothers and looks back at the saloon owner. "You have any thoughts on this?" Tuck knits his fingers thoughtfully through the long whiskers on his chin and shrugs. "Jest wondering if you were going to make it to the Barrelhouse for the performance tonight?"

Chapter 15

The street is cast in shadows as evening settles and lantern lights are brought out to illuminate the wide boardwalk and front porch of the building that serves as Tuck's Barrelhouse. The flaming glow of the oil lamps makes the saloon stand out among the lineup of shabby, worn-down wooden structures. The visiting performer has attracted a small crowd nearly rivaled by the shooting incident earlier in the week, as a varied assembly of townsfolk comes out of hiding to watch the night's entertainment.

Everett steps past the milling individuals on the front porch and enters the saloon, where a lineup of chairs surrounds a small stage. The lawman scans the room and spots Tuck leaned over the bar slab speaking to someone standing opposite. Stepping toward the rear of the saloon, Everett proceeds to where the evening's host holds court.

Tuck stands behind the expanse of bar and glances over as Everett approaches. "Marshal... Sure glad you made it."

"Hope this show is more entertainin' than the one you put on earlier, Tuckburrow."

The saloon owner takes a cigar from his vest pocket, tosses it between his teeth and grins. "You never know when life will get excitin'." Tuck's eyes light up with apparent mischief, as Charlotte steps up behind Everett at the bar rail.

"Marshal, I believe you've become somewhat acquainted with my lady-friend, Miss Torres?"

Everett instinctively touches the badge on his vest to find it still there and turns to regard Charlotte's icy stare with a tip of his hat. "Yes, we have met."

A flare of indignation flushes her made-up features. She turns to leave but is brought back by Tuck reaching out, grabbing her arm and whispering hoarsely over the bar top. "Hold on there, Darlin'. Take a seat 'n watch the show... Don't be rude." Tuck pulls her closer to them and smirks toward Everett. "She's still a mite sore that she couldn't comfortably perform her horse riding routine this morning." Tuck grins teasingly and smoothes his chin whiskers down as Charlotte gives him a stern, unamused glare.

Gazing around at the crowd-filled bar room, Everett notices Marlow, the bartender, moving toward them as his brothers situate themselves near the entry doors to observe. The bartender makes his way through the saloon and leans over the bar top to convey a secretive message to Tuckburrow. Perturbed, Tuck listens, tilts his head and motions Marlow to his position behind the bar before turning to address Everett. "Our main attraction is being detained down in the livery. Care to join me, Marshal?"

The saloon owner pours them both a shot of whiskey. Tuck lifts his tumbler and downs the drink in one swallow. Everett nods his thanks, takes a sip and notices the saloon owner cover his frock coat over his holstered sidearm while sliding the other smaller hideaway pistol into his waistband. Tuck looks across at Charlotte and gives her a broad wink. "Git that sore bottom of yourn seated darlin', we'll be back."

Everett moves through the milling crowd and follows Tuck toward the door. They stop at the front entryway which is flanked by Vic and Ben. Everett offers them a quiet nod and he motions for Tuck to proceed outside. "After you, sir."

Tuck tips his chin courteously toward the watchful deputies and proceeds out the double doors to the boardwalk. A word is exchanged between the brothers, and Tuck stops at the stairway. He turns to look over his shoulder as Everett follows behind and then gives the lawman a rascally grin. "Didn't I tell you the evenin' could get a mite entertainin'?"

~*~

Tuck and Everett walk on the far side of the street from the lighted front of the saloon toward the dark end of town. They move past a vacant plot of frontage with the charred remains from a burnt-out building. Tuck stops to twist the cigar in his mouth, takes a match from his vest pocket and strikes it with his thumbnail. The flare from the lit stick glows against his features and his eyes dart over to the fire-destroyed building. "The Barrelhouse was once here."

The flame of the match fades into the orange fiery tip of the cigar, and Tuck exhales out a white cloud of smoke. Standing beside each other in the street, the saloon owner turns his narrowed gaze to study the lawman's reaction. In the moonlit shadows, Everett observes how the few remaining burnt pieces of lumber almost seem to form a somber gallows. "Had you a fire, did ya?"

Tuck blows another puff of smoke, his eyes twinkling. "T'was no accidental fire. Damned arsonists, jest up 'n burned me out one night."

Everett looks behind them at the new location of the barrelhouse and the bright lamps glowing from the porch. "Know who it was?"

Tuck nods and twists the damp, cut end of the cigar between his lips. "Oh, yeah. Still owe 'em fer it too." The saloon owner stands, smoking his cigar in the faint moonlight and contemplates the resonating remains of the former saloon. "The thing is, I had a hell of a fine ol' time putting this saloon together and gettin' myself a firm toehold in this burg with it. This no account, one-horse stop wasn't always a ghost town."

"What happened to it?"

Tuck takes the cigar from his mouth and ashes it. "Someone started stepping on toes."

Everett looks away from the foreboding structure over to Tuckburrow. "Prosperity is often followed by greed."

In the darkness, Tuck turns around to face to Everett. His features reflect a fiery light, as he replaces the cigar between his lips and takes a long drag. "Tyranny is the result of too much power."

Everett watches Tuck as the glow from the cigar flickers in his eyes. "You figure it was the Werners?"

Tuck puffs the small cigar and it burns brightly. "You've stepped in the midst of a bad situation 'round here." A wisp of smoke escapes through his mustache as he speaks. "Keeping to the middle-ground is a dangerous place to be." Tuck takes the cigar from his teeth, exhales and smirks. "Dutch Werner and some of his cow hands are in the stables jest o'er yonder, itching for a fight. They burned me out once and are more'n ready to stomp someone tonight."

Everett puts a palm to the holstered pistol on his hip and his coat lapel slides back to reveal a corner of the badge. "My kin and I know our business here and will stick to it."

Tuck takes a drag from the lit tobacco and blows out a cloud of hazy smoke as he wipes his lip, grinning in the moonlight. He shrugs apathetically, as he steps toward the livery barn with Everett at his side. "We'll see about yer stickin' to business. Figure I don't have to advise you 'bout keeping yer back to the wall with these folks?" Tuck takes a final drag on his cigar and tosses it aside.

Chapter 16

The barn and corrals are illuminated by dingy oil lamps hanging from wooden pegs on hand-hewn support beams. The muted glow of light lets out a plume of heavy smoke from wicks turned up high. Gathered in the aisle of the barn, between stalls, are several cowboys with Jenks and Curtis. Actor, J.M. Lucas the III sits perched on a pile of loose straw, with a whiskey bottle in each hand staring out the barn door. "Well, hello there Mister Tuckburrow..."

The lamplight shines on Everett and Tuck as they appear in the wide doorway to the livery to scrutinize the crowd of cowboys. A quick assessment reveals the numbers to be not in their favor but the odds not terribly overwhelming. Tuck steps into the barn, advances to the pile of livestock bedding and snatches a sloshing bottle from the seated actor. He tips it back to take a nip and shakes his head at the actor. "You've had enough there, fella..."

Jenks reaches out and roughly grabs Tuck's shoulder. "Hey there, leave him be... He was going to do us a show." Tuck glimpses the hand gripped on his coat, then glares at Jenks and replies, "Buy a ticket." The ranch foreman clamps his hand firmly on the saloon owner's shoulder as his other fist begins to curl and swing forward. In a flash of movement, Tuck twists away and smashes the bottle across Jenks' face.

Whiskey and broken glass splash to the straw-covered floor as Jenks staggers a few steps and then crumples against a wood-slat corral. Tuck turns to confront the others and suddenly has a pistol in hand with the hammer pulled back. Positioning his backside to one of the beam support posts, Tuck nudges the actor from the low pile of straw. With effort, he helps the drunken performer to his feet and attempts to steady him under the arm.

The other whiskey bottle falls from the actor's hand and rolls away, as all eyes are on Tuck and his cocked pistol. J.M. Lucas wavers drunkenly on his feet, as Tuck levels the barrel of his pistol at the remaining lineup of *D/W* cowhands. A snide grimace appears beneath his long, uncut moustache, as Tuck's watchful gaze darts to the slumped figure of Jenks, who rolls and moans pitifully. The saloon owner grumbles, "Sorry 'bout laying out ol' Jenks there, but feel free to step up and get a lead cavity for yer trouble."

Curtis seems completely gobsmacked as he gawks down at Jenks on the plank-wood floor and then across the barn at Tuck, who assists the intoxicated actor toward the barn exit. "You squirrelly son of a bitch! You can't do that."

Tuck turns the aim of his firearm to Curtis and grins. "How-so? I just done it." Tuck raises his pistol barrel slightly to eliminate any question of his intentions. "Won't you be a good fellow and come watch the show with everyone else?" Tuck steps back to where Everett waits at the barn opening. After receiving no further threats from the group of cowboys, he uncocks his handgun with a series of clicks and brashly tilts his bearded chin toward Everett as he holsters his gun. "See there? That's the way you have to deal with 'em."

The rancher's son fumes with anger and redirects his focus to the lawman standing at the door. "Hey, you're the new marshal in town. You gonna let him do that?"

Everett steps aside and gives a wide berth as Tuck supports the drunken actor on his shoulder at the doorway. "You may go." He turns to Curtis, fronting the other cowboys and gestures to Jenks. "Get your man and take him home."

"Whose side you on, law-dog?"

Everett stands between the two opposing factions, glancing from the group of angered cowboys over to Tuck. "Just standin' in the middle."

Tuck grunts with amusement and cracks a big smile. "Hate to tell ya, but there ain't room for jest goin' halfway." The exiting saloon owner casts his gaze over at Curtis, standing with his hired hands, and gives him a snarky wink. "Be seein' you another time *rancher-boy*." The smug comment from Tuck is more than the hotheaded cowboy can stand.

Curtis jerks his pistol out, cocks the hammer and points it at Tuck. Everett instantly slaps his palm to his sidearm, slides it clear from the holster and calls to the rancher's son, "Hold it now!"

The cocked and ready pistol directed at Tuck begins to tremble slightly as Curtis tries to contain his boiling rage. "Tuck, you sonovabitch!"

Everett sternly gazes down his outstretched arm to the rancher's son lined up in his gunsights. "Put down that gun, or I will put you down."

Curtis looks from the saloon owner to the lawman and attempts to comprehend the terse warning. The tense situation seems to be in limbo until the drunk actor stumbles forward, waves both hands in front of him and speaks with a slur, "Gentlemen, there is no need to be fighting..."

The standstill ends when Curtis lowers his pistol and the firearm's cocked hammer accidentally trips forward with an exploding gun-blast. The fiery muzzle of the pistol flashes to ignite the straw bedding at his feet as the stray bullet strikes and bounces from the floor. Everett keeps his firearm pointed in the direction of the cowboys and turns to see if Tuck is hit.

Standing outside the door, Tuck quickly assesses he is unharmed and grins smugly at Curtis. "I see ya cain't hit the broad side of a barn from the inside!"

The actor lets out a dramatic, gasping moan and slumps to his knees in front of Tuck. He clutches his hurt chest and slowly crumples to the ground. Curtis steps forward while lowering his pistol and stammers, "I didn't mean to shoot 'im... I was gunnin' for Tuck."

Everett swings his handgun around and whacks Curtis solidly across the crown. The broad-brimmed Stetson on the pistol-whipped victim goes askew and the rancher's son drops to the barn floor in a dazed heap. Everett quickly returns his pistol's aim to the cowboys behind and calls out forcefully, "Keep back, you there!"

At the dimly lit barn entry, Tuck kneels beside the wounded actor and props him up against his bended knee. Wheezing for breath, J.M. Lucas rolls his eyes around to the haloed light of the hanging oil lamps. "Am I in heaven yet?"

Tuck sniffs and shakes his head, "Not exactly..."

Everett reaches down, grabs Curtis by the shirt collar and drags him toward the doorway. He pauses as the actor continues to passionately express himself in gasping pants.

"*Marched the brave from rocky steep, from mountain-river swift and cold; the borders of the stormy deep, the values where gathered waters sleep, Sent up the strong and bold, -* "

Everett stares at the performer, in a blood-stained shirt, clutching at the front of his brocade vest with clenched fist. The lawman glances down at Curtis, who remains in a daze, and speaks to Tuck in a low voice. "Best get him the doctor." Tuck shakes his head dejectedly as he watches the actor spout his final performance with his last dying breath.

"As if the very earth again grew quick with God's creating breath, And from the sods of grove and glen, Rose the ranks of lion-hearted men to battle to the death."

The fatally wounded performer seems to get the last few poetic verses out just before his final curtain call. Bloodshot and whiskey-soaked eyes cover over and slow-fluttering lids usher the freeing release of his soul to eternity. Tuck looks up at Everett and lets the empty shell of the actor's earthly bound form gently settle to the straw-covered floor. He heaves a heavy-hearted breath and murmurs aloud, "Always wondered 'bout the way them actors retired."

Everett retains his collared grip on the half-conscious Curtis and shoves him outside the livery barn doorway. "Tuckburrow, do me a favor and take him to the jailhouse."

The pistol-whipped rancher's son seems to regain a bit of his facilities and slowly climbs to his feet. The saloon owner takes Curtis under the arm and turns to the town marshal. "You want to think you're still in the middle?"

Everett scans the lineup of *D/W* brand cowboys across from them in the barn, keeping his gun pointed at waist level. They stare back at the two with a cold hostility in their gaze. Everett remains warily silent, as Tuck answers his own query. "I think everyone else has formed a different opinion."

Chapter 17

The evening street outside the livery barn is dark and silent. Behind Everett, at the far end of the town, Tuck's saloon is still doing energetic business in anticipation of the night's show. His gun still leveled at the line-up of cowboys, Everett calls past his shoulder to the street without glancing back at Tuck. "Get him out of here and send the Chinaman for this one." Everett takes another step to the open door and nudges the deceased actor with his boot heel.

Tuck supports the dazed body of Curtis and grunts, "The undertaker is the busiest fella in town all of a sudden." He heaves the pistol-thumped cowboy higher to be supported by his shoulder and proceeds down the empty, moonlit street. The occupants of the barn all remain quiet as the scuffling of dragging feet fades out toward the marshal's office.

Everett stands inside the barn door with his pistol still raised and the cowboys begin to grumble with discontent. They notice Jenks slowly rousing to his senses against the side of the corral and Everett gestures toward him with his pistol. "Go ahead and tend to him if you want." The cowboys drag the half-conscious body of Jenks along the floor and place him across the pile of straw where the actor was once seated. Everett slowly backs further out the door around the dead performer and into the street.

He holsters his sidearm, turns and suddenly comes face to face with the dark, shadowed features of Dutch Werner. The two remain in a silent standoff waiting for the other to make a move. The old rancher finally steps into the livery barn and stands before Everett. "Hello there," he looks to the star-shaped law-badge still pinned on Everett's chest and narrows his eyes, "...Marshal."

"Evening, Dutch."

They stand, face to face, with the rancher purposefully hindering the lawman's exit. Dutch lets his gaze drop to the dead body at their feet and then glimpses over Everett's shoulder to the slumped form of Jenks sitting on the loose pile of straw. He steps aside from the barn doorway and mutters, in a low tone, "Oh, excuse me... Did I interrupt something?"

Everett keeps his open palm near the handle of his sidearm and peers back at Jenks and the group of cowboys. "They'll have a version of the doin's different from mine."

Dutch glances at the deceased actor and snidely retorts, "I heard there was to be a show tonight. Guess I missed it."

The lawman stands his ground before the menacing rancher and responds. "I doubt you miss much."

Dutch puts on a wolfish grin and produces a flask from his coat pocket. "Can I offer you a drink?"

Everett relaxes his arm but still seems ready to draw at the least provocation. "Maybe another time." He dips the brim of his hat to Dutch and steps cautiously away to the street.

Dutch Werner waits, takes note of the footsteps striding away, then turns and marches into the barn's full lamplight. The cowboys keep silent as their boss' demeanor morphs from calmness to fury. He violently swings one of the large barn doors closed and it bounces and rattles the hinges after hitting the dead actor's body in the doorway. "You damned assheads! What the hell's wrong with you?"

Jenks peers up at his boss and wipes the damp whiskey and bits of glass from his vest. "They got the bulge on us."

Dutch scans the submissive assembly of cowboys and bellows, "Who ya say done it? There were only two of 'em!"

One of the cowboys speaks up and gestures to the body of J.M. Lucas in the barn entry. "…and that drunken actor."

The rancher swings a hammered fist to the jaw of the cowboy who tumbles against the corral. "Who else is canny?"

Dutch walks to Jenks and looms over him ominously. "Least my damned boy Curtis there had a bit of sand in 'im. You worthless egg-suckers should 'a backed him and shot the hell out of them two!" Jenks touches the sore side of his head and pulls a piece of broken, whiskey bottle glass from his hair. He opens his mouth to speak and Dutch reels back his hand. "Don't even say it, or I'll lay you out worse than what you got already." The angry rancher's eyes turn and stare hard at each of his hired hands. "Now we have to get Curtis clear of this. The next time we come in contest with them newly-appointed lawmen, I want lead to fly. Got it?"

Jenks waves over one of the hands to help him to his feet, and the chastised group of cowboys shuffle to the partly closed door, heading outside to their mounts in the corral. Dutch Werner unsympathetically watches them all exit the livery barn, as he stands in the flickering light of the oil lamp. He waits awhile and listens as the cowboys climb into their saddles, trot down the street and ride away.

Dutch walks over to a stack of tools leaned on the wall, picks up a long-handled shovel and weighs the manure-crusted blade in his hands. A brief glance to the body in the doorway and a manic-rage fills his matured, craggy features. The rancher swings the shovel in a long arc through the air and the flat blade smashes the oil lamp in a splash of light, fading the barn's interior to darkness.

Chapter 18

A whirlwind of dust travels through the daytime streets of the town while Everett sits on the marshal's office front stoop. His squinted eyes travel the length of abandoned buildings, observing not a soul present in any of them. The rattle of a loose window pane is heard from one of the old structures, and Everett turns his gaze out beyond the town limits to the surrounding vacant landscape.

The door behind Everett pulls to the inside with a sliding scrape, and Vic steps past the office entry threshold. The elder brother chews on a thin stick of wood and gazes out to the town. "What are we gonna do with him?"

Vic hooks his thumb over his shoulder toward the jail cell in back and Everett continues to stare out at the seemingly abandoned burg. The two brothers are silent until Everett finally lets out a breath. "We'll just hold 'im in there a bit."

Vic peers down at his brother. "Then what?"

The two remain quiet, as a slight gusting breeze raises the layer of dirt along the boardwalk into a swirling of dust. Everett turns partly in the chair and gazes up at his brother. "So far, Dutch Werner and his cowpokes had no reason to take the matter serious or own up to their wrongful misdeed." Vic nods while picking his teeth, and Everett continues, "Having that one in there gets them to thinking."

The older brother finishes with the chewed toothpick, flicks it out into the empty street and scratches above his ear. "Most likely he's the one who done it anyhow."

"That is my thought, too."

Vic adjusts the position of his hat on his head and pats Everett on the shoulder. "There's not much of a chance for the circuit judge to pass through this no-name town without sending word 'forhand."

"No evidence to put 'gainst him either."

"Hell, you saw him shoot that actor fellow."

"T'was an accident. He meant to shoot Tuck."

Vic grunts and continues to gaze out to the street. "Dead is dead."

Everett stares ahead and extends his boots before him. "All we have is my word with the questionable reputation of the saloon owner against half a dozen of his cowboy friends." Everett lifts a booted foot and crosses it over at his ankle. "They need to pay for what they done to our kin, not some soused actor."

Vic grunts and glances back inside the office at Curtis. "It won't make the law no never mind."

"And it won't come to anything with a judge... especially if Dutch Werner owns 'im."

"Yeah, not much seems to happen around here that Dutch don't have a hand in." Vic taps dirt from the side of his boot against the door frame. He narrows his eyes to the figure in the jail cell at the back of the office and pulls the door shut. "That fella back there is just workin' off the day's hangover." The older brother looks down at his younger sibling, then he gazes out to the empty street and the Barrelhouse beyond. "You okay to stick 'round here 'n watch him while I go across the way and work on makin' one of my own?"

"Sure, go on Vic. He ain't going anywhere."

Along to Presidio

Vic moves forward, steps down from the boardwalk and turns in the street. He glances up at his brother and grins. "Be good, little brother. Don't go takin' on the world all by yerself now, ya hear?" Everett puts a finger to the brim of his pushed back hat and salutes his sibling. The eldest of the Colbert brothers nods affirmative and steps across the street to the Barrelhouse saloon.

~*~

The line of shadows cast from the hitching rail slowly travel, like a sundial, around the upright post, as Everett partly dozes in the chair on the porch of the marshal's office. The faraway nicker of a horse rouses him from his slumber, and he looks to see a single-rigged carriage approaching. Everett removes his Stetson hat, rubs the sleep from his eyes and pushes his hair back before returning the felt hat to its position on his head.

A ways down the street, a four wheeled buggy rolls along behind a high-stepping, lathered up steed in harness. Everett attempts to make out the identity of the individual driver and stands to get a better vantage. He steps forward and leans on the porch support post as the carriage with the double bench seat rolls closer.

To Everett's surprise, a female driver steers the buggy in front of the marshal's office and halts the reined animal. Sitting to the middle of the spring-supported bench seat, with a horsehide blanket covering over her lap, sits the young woman from the stagecoach incident days prior. She gazes up at Everett, standing in the porch shadow, and nods.

Everett seems a bit astonished at her liberated presence. He looks behind at her back-trail of unaccompanied wheel tracks for some sort of protecting escort and is dumbfounded. The young lady glances up at the marshal and sets the lead lines aside, as she turns back the covering over her lap. "Excuse me sir. What town is this?"

The young woman straightens her skirting over her ankle boots and pats the trail dust from her shirt sleeve. Everett watches her with interest and stammers, "Yes, Miss, uh, no Miss, I surely don't know."

Shel looks at him confused. "What don't you know?"

"This town really doesn't have a name... Miss?"

"Adeline Sonnett."

Everett steps down from the wooden boardwalk, approaches the horse drawn buggy and then removes his hat. "Am pleased to meet you, Miss Sonnett." She looks over at him and smiles a warm greeting. Looking into her bright eyes, he can't get over his wonder. "Are you alone?"

Adeline continues her smile at Everett and shrugs innocently. "It is often hard to find anywhere to be alone... But yes, at this particular moment, I am unaccompanied."

"That's not really safe 'round these parts."

"Are you referring to the well-being of the stagecoach or just the wild frontier in general?"

Everett thinks back on their recent encounter and the hostile territory, days prior. "Well, yes ... both."

Adeline lifts the covering blanket from the seat beside her to reveal a nickel-plated six-gun. She pats the revolver and shrugs at the judgmental treatment. "I decided to reinvest my stagecoach funds on this horse rig and a frontier six-shooter."

Everett seems clearly impressed with her fortitude, but unconvinced of her safety. "That's a fine looking weapon for protection, but do you know how to load and use that thing?"

She stares earnestly across the few feet between them and frowns. "Well enough to hit my mark from here, sir."

Everett nods with a skeptical squinted eye and replies, "Sometimes it can take a bit more than squeezing a trigger."

Adeline covers the gun with the blanket and curiously gazes out past her harness animal into the one-horse town. "This is the second time we have chanced upon each other. May I ask, what is your name?"

"Everett Colbert."

She looks to the metal star pinned on Everett's vest and raises an eyebrow. "And you're a lawman?"

"Uh, yes… along with my brothers."

Adeline looks Everett over, as he stands along the boardwalk and lets his coat lapel cover over the star-badge. "On our first encounter, you didn't advertise to anyone that you were a man of the law."

"It happened recent." The two study each other curiously until Everett turns his gaze to the items of luggage behind the buggy seat bench. "Can I be of assistance with those bags or your horse rig?"

Adeline turns and looks to the oddly empty town. "Well, Mister Law-in-Town, if there is a hotel or livery stable, it would be nice if you would point me in the right direction."

Everett points across the street to the decrepit hotel. "Not much to choose from, but that place has rooms to rent. Livery is down at the end of the street."

The animal in the buggy-rig harness cocks a leg and lowers its neck to rest, as the dusty breeze blows into its face. Everett angles his head against the wind to keep his hat, and Adeline tilts her face down, covering her hand over her eyes. The short gusting breeze passes momentarily, and the two remain alone in the street of the seemingly uninhabited town. Everett extends his hand up for her climb down and waits. "Let me assist you."

The lawman helps her from the buggy, and Adeline nods her appreciation. She moves around behind the rear wheel and unlashes the line of rope secured over her luggage.

Opening one of her bags, Adeline takes the pistol from the bench and places it inside before buckling it closed again. Everett steps beside her. "Let me help you with those."

Adeline grips the handles of her bag and holds firm. She peers at the lawman with a strong air of independence. "I've been carrying my own baggage for quite some time without much trouble, thank you very much."

Everett seems enthralled by her self-reliance, as she heaves the luggage from the carriage and stands before him. He steps back and utters, "How long do you plan to stay?"

"Are you asking as a *lawman* or as an acquaintance?"

Everett looks down at his law-badge partly concealed by his coat and smiles. "I'd like to be your friend, Miss."

"Perhaps I will be around a day or two."

Watching Adeline handle herself with the luggage, Everett recognizes her prettiness and autonomous gumption. "I can't help but wonder why you would choose to stop here."

Adeline turns toward the hotel and assesses it acutely. "So, why did you?"

Unaccustomed to inquisitive retorts, Everett replies, "We had an unfortunate incident and are seeking reparation."

Adeline turns back to Everett and lets her sparkling gaze connect with his. "I am looking for something, as well."

Mystified by this woman, the lawman glances around the town before asking, "And what might that be?"

Everett studies Adeline and senses the strong feelings of emotion come over her countenance, "Or who perhaps?" She then utters the familiar name, "Hollister Tuckburrow."

Almost losing his composure, Everett hesitantly asks, "Do you mean, Tuck?"

Adeline tilts her head to Everett inquiringly and rolls her shoulder from the weight of the bags. "If he is indeed here in this town, I would like to surprise Mister Tuckburrow."

The lawman nods toward the other side of the street. "He owns the Barrelhouse across the way."

"Then, I'm in the right place."

Everett adjusts his gaze as he notices Marlow, the bartender, step out into the shadows under the porch of the saloon and look his way. "Well, I don't know 'bout that." Adeline turns from her consideration of the hotel and takes in the saloon structure, Tuck's Barrelhouse, situated next door. Everett steps up alongside her and reiterates his offer to help with her luggage. "Can I carry one of those for you?"

"No."

"How about I take your rig to the livery?"

She nods her consent, and Everett twirls a hand forward toward the old hotel. "Joe Evans is the proprietor of rooms and should give you a decent stay." He climbs onto the carriage, takes the reins and gets situated on the bench seat. "The rooms aren't much, but he claims to keep 'em clean."

Adeline turns to look at Everett, and her eyes drop down to the law-badge on his vest. "Thank you, Marshal."

"Miss Sonnett. Please call me Everett."

Adeline sets down her heavy baggage in the dirt street and extends her gloved hand to the lawman. "Fine... Everett, you may call me Adeline."

He drops the leather harness reins to his lap, takes her feminine hand respectfully and tilts his head with a bow. "Pleased to make your acquaintance, Adeline."

She blushes slightly and removes her hand from his. "Please do remember our secret... I want to surprise him."

Everett reaffirms with a nod, as he watches her grab up her bags of luggage and saunter across the street to the hotel. He whistles slightly under his breath and then mutters aloud, "Oh, he should be surprised alright."

Chapter 19

The afternoon sunlight slants across the floor of the marshal's office through cracks in the wood door and shutter windows. A rope-slung cot is positioned along the wall opposite the desk, and Everett lays back, seemingly asleep. He has a knee propped against the adobe bricks and peeks out from beneath the hat over his forehead, as the thumping of cowboy boots is heard on the boardwalk outside.

The heavy front door of the office unlatches and slowly swings open with a low, groaning creak of rusty hinges. Everett observes from under the brim as his younger brother, Ben, enters the room and lets his eyes adjust to the low light. Without sitting up, Everett eases his hand away from something under a folded blanket and speaks out a greeting. "Hello there, Ben."

Ben swings the door shut to see Everett on the bunk and then peers into the rear jail cell where Curtis sits against the wall. "Hey brother, has he been giving you any trouble?"

Everett glances out from under the raised brim of his hat at their prisoner and replies, "Not a peep." Ben opens one of the gun-port window shutters to let in the afternoon light, and the rope framework under the bunk mattress creaks as Everett sits up to pull a pistol from under the blanket.

Ben watches and smiles fondly at his older brother. "What's with the hideaway?"

"I little habit I learned from someone."

Ben stares at Everett with interest but doesn't receive further explanation, so he resumes gazing out the window. "Anything new happening here in town?"

"Not much. Vic is having a drink across the street."

Ben looks back and smiles again. "Official business?"

Everett shakes out his boots, pulls them on and rises to his feet. "We figure, if we keep that one back there a while, they will eventually come to us." The two brothers stand beside each other at the window, looking across the street at Tuck's Barrelhouse and the decrepit hotel building next door. Ben rests a hand on the wall with the other on his holster belt. "I watched them all day in the valley yonder, and they didn't appear to move any of our stock in with theirs."

"Might be they won't work them together."

"That was one of the many ideas that crossed my mind, sittin' out there in the hot sun."

"They must figure we'll be watching their every move for a while, so they might just be playing it careful for now. They'll show their hand sooner or later."

Ben nods somberly as he gazes into the empty street. "The kicker is I don't really care so much about them cattle, now that Uncle Jacque is gone." Everett remains quiet as he stares out the window at the Barrelhouse and then the hotel. Ben shakes his head and looks back to the occupied jail cell. "How many of these cowboys do we have to even the score with to make it feel right?"

Everett narrows is hard gaze and tilts his hat forward. "It ain't ever gonna feel right."

~*~

The late-day, orange beams of sunshine stream in through the dusty front window panels of Tuck's Barrelhouse. A figure outside the saloon mounts the front porch steps and approaches the double doorway with a light tentative foot. The feminine silhouette, outfitted in a slim-fitting jacket and long, riding skirt pushes the double entry doors open with the sunlight streaming in from behind.

At the entrance to the saloon, Adeline gazes around the room, searchingly studying the unfamiliar selection of faces. The occupants of the drinking establishment all turn to stare at the newcomer before slowly returning to their prior task. The busy din of the room returns as Adeline steps inside.

At the back of the room, Charlotte hangs out near the door to the cribs and rear exit as she observes the newcomer. She seems taken aback at the nerve of the audacious woman stepping into the saloon unescorted and approaching the bar. Marlow swipes a clean towel across the polished bar-top and, with a friendly smile, stands across the slab from Adeline. "Miss, there's no need for you to be standing like the menfolk. Can I seat you at one of the tables near the windows?"

Marlow motions to the unoccupied tables at the front of the room, away from the hazy smoke and gambling chatter. Adeline glances around the populated saloon and notices the probing stare of a man observing her from the gaming table. The badge-wearing deputy looks around the card table and takes the cigar from the mouth of the man seated beside him.

Vic smiles kindly toward Adeline, as he deposits the smoking stub of rolled tobacco into the nearest mug of beer. The still-lit cigar sizzles out in the unfinished drink, and the gambler's shocked expression is rebuked by a frown from Vic. The deputy offers a friendly salute toward Adeline, and she returns the gesture with a slight nod.

She addresses Marlow behind the bar with a smile, "No, thanks. A drink here will be fine." The bartender looks down the length of the bar at several patrons and the woman glaring at them from the far end. "But, Miss... It's not proper."

"Sir, if I did everything that was proper I would still be sipping tea in Pennsylvania." Adeline puts a palm to the edge of the bar top and looks around until she catches Charlotte's unwelcoming stare. "A local beer would be just fine for me." Marlow's jaw hangs down slack as he stutters in wonderment, "A… a beer? Miss, I do have some very fine wines imported from France, Europe that I think you might really enjoy."

Adeline turns to face the bartender and smiles kindly. "For now, a beer would be fine, sir."

Acquiescing with a bow, Marlow turns and grabs up his fanciest glass to fill at the keg. Charlotte scoots closer along the rail and leans over the top toward the bartender and whispers in a hissing tone, "What does she want here?"

Marlow peeks over his arm at the questioning woman and continues the task of a careful pour. "She wants a beer."

The garishly dressed saloon entertainer glares down the slab at the newcomer in ordinary, feminine trail clothes. Her stare travels down to notice a pair of dusty riding boots poking out from under the long hem of the coarse cotton skirt. Charlotte turns back to Marlow and continues to speak low. "Who does she think she is, and what is she doing here?"

Marlow finishes the pour and paddles the beer foam from the rim of the glass. He speaks over his shoulder at her, not attempting to disguise the annoyed tone in his voice. "Charlotte, I don't have any idea why she is here. Why don't you try to be a mite friendlier and go ask her yourself?" Charlotte shrewdly watches as the doting bartender carefully carries the beer-filled glass to the waiting female customer. Moving gradually closer, she casually slides her hand down the bar rail as she strains to overhear the exchange and makes a sour face at Marlow's obedient and courteous attentions. "Miss… My name is Marlow. If there is anything you need, you just let me know."

Marlow bends low to bow and gives a harsh look at Charlotte, as she slides her way down the length of bar-top. She returns his critical frown with a smirk and approaches the perceived threat of a woman in the saloon. Charlotte sidles up to Adeline and feigns a welcoming tone, *"Buenas dias Señorita. Mi nombre es Charlotte Torres."*

Adeline turns to face Charlotte and takes in her bright, flaming red hair and glimmering eyes that shine, icy blue. "Hello Miss Torres, I'm pleased to make your acquaintance." Charlotte is momentarily caught off guard by Adeline's open, friendly manner and leans a bit closer to her at the bar rail. She speaks in a hushed, rasping tone as if to uncover a secret. "Who are you and why are you here?"

Adeline raises the fancy glass of beer to take a short sip. "I am Adeline Sonnett, and as you know, I am new in town." Charlotte looks around the crowded barroom and reassures herself that there isn't anyone taking notice of them at the bar. "Not a soul comes here without a purpose. What's yours? ...Are you looking for someone?" Adeline studies the woman beside her in fancy, entertainer fashions and then turns to gaze out the window. "Yes... Yes, I am."

Charlotte glances around again to assess if anyone is listening and then leans in to whisper insightfully to Adeline. "Is it a certain gentleman that has come with his brothers?"

Adeline curiously peers at Charlotte over the rim of her glass of beer. "Do you mean the marshal?"

The recreational lady seems haughty in her perceived knowledge of the goings on in town. "Sí. Is he who you seek?"

Adeline shakes her head and gazes around the room. "No. It's another man whom I have known a long time."

Charlotte pauses as she contemplates the scenario. "Señorita, I know most everyone who comes to this pueblo, but maybe my fiancé can help you find who you are seeking." She grins knowingly, "He knows all that goes on and everybody from here to Mexico."

Seeming to understand, Adeline looks to Marlow, watching them from the other end of the bar, then looks back at Charlotte. "Yes. He is your fiancé?"

Charlotte follows Adeline's gaze to the bartender and shakes her head while rudely laughing and snorting out loud, "No, no, no... He is just a mere tender of this old cantina. Señor Tuck will one day take my hand in matrimony."

Adeline tries to contain her enthusiasm at hearing the long, sought after name. "You mean, Hollister Tuckburrow?"

Charlotte gives a snooty smirk, flips her bright, flowing hair over her shoulder and grins wide. "The one and only."

With eyes set on her barroom companion, Adeline lifts her fancy beer glass and takes a tiny sip from the glass rim. "Would you perhaps do me the great honor of allowing me to buy you a drink, Miss Torres?"

Charlotte is momentarily distracted from Adeline's eloquent banter, as she turns her attention to the front entry. The sound of several stomping boots on the boardwalk stairs thumps nearer as two figures walk through the beaming haze of light that streams in the double front doors and windows. Adeline follows her gaze, turning to witness the appearance of the town marshal followed by a familiar face from the past, veiled behind a shaggy, uncut beard.

Chapter 20

The ordinary sounds of the saloon quickly fade away as an electric tingle of exhilaration charges through Adeline's body. It only takes a moment for her to identify the long-sought after image of Hollister Tuckburrow. With a tinge of suspicion, Charlotte watches Adeline scrutinize Tuck as he enters the room behind the marshal and proceed to the length of bar. Her jealous gaze begins to narrow, questioning the other woman's motives and prior association.

The two men lean on the bar rail, nearest the doorway and Tuck takes his hat off and slaps it down on the bar top. He lets his eyes scan the customers in the room as he hollers, "Marlow, set us up!" Tuck halts his perusing gaze when he recognizes Adeline and suddenly appears frozen with dismay. Beside him at the rail of the bar, Everett watches, intrigued, as the gregarious saloon owner stands momentarily agape.

Adeline directs her attentions to the front of the saloon, near the door, and takes another sip from the glass of beer. She inhales a calming breath before setting it down with a soft clunk and steps out into the barroom to face Tuckburrow. "Hello Hollister... It's been a long time." Tuck swallows hard but remains stationary, as she takes a step toward him. Beginning to seem somewhat unsure of her surprise reunion, Adeline directs her gaze to Everett. "Hello Marshal."

Everett graciously tips the brim of his hat to Adeline and seems to enjoy the uncomfortable meeting of the young female and saloon owner. There is an expectant pause as the two figures stare at each other. He finally nudges Tuck from the side and gestures to the woman standing before them. "You have anything to say to the lady?"

Tuck blinks, finally seeming to regain his senses, and then turns from Adeline to Everett. "What is she doing here?" Everett extends an elbow to the bar and his brow crinkles under the brim of his hat. He looks past Tuck to Adeline. "That's a hell of a question for me. Ask her yourself."

In the ensuing lull, Charlotte moves closer to the awkward encounter and imposes herself in the conversation. "Who is this girl, Tuck?" She turns her shoulder away from Adeline and leans closer to Tuck. "Why has she come here?"

Tuck is suddenly mindful again and glares at Charlotte. "You keep quiet... It's none of your damned business."

The saloon entertainer's animated features flush red with humiliation and her crimson hair pales by comparison. Charlotte heaves her chest in anger and spits her words with the malice of a woman scorned. "Tuck, I am to be your wife!" Her gaze travels from Everett to Adeline and back to Tuck. "Some stranger woman shows herself in town for you, and you say to me this is not my damned business?"

Tuck stands facing Adeline and is at a loss for words. He gulps a lungful of air, shakes his head with a groan and turns to march toward the entry doors, swinging them wide. As the saloon owner steps outside to the front porch, Charlotte murmurs livid curses under her breath after him. There is an air of emptiness in the room, as the saloon doors slowly swing closed and Adeline turns to address Charlotte. "My sincere apologies to you, Miss Torres. Please know that Mister Tuckburrow was someone I was once very close to."

The fancily-dressed recreational woman calms herself, looks Adeline over and gives a snide huff. "Doesn't matter. He's a low-life degenerate, rat-bastard scoundrel anyway." Adeline ignores Charlotte's spiteful outburst and proceeds to step out the entrance after Tuck.

The saloon entertainer moves to follow them outside and Everett reaches out, grabbing her by the arm to stop her. "Hold on there, *Red*, I told you to watch that tongue of yourn. You go out there, and we'll have us another round." The town marshal gives a wink and slaps his open palm on his thigh.

Charlotte whirls her head to stare daggers at Everett. She tears her arm away from his hold and backpedals down the length of the room toward the rear section of the saloon. "You lascivious menfolk are always the same... There is forever someone fresher or prettier who gets your attention." She reaches over the bar to grab herself a bottle and continues to stare toward the front entry as she reveals ample cleavage. Standing upright, Charlotte snarls at the lawman with a hiss, "You will all end up dying alone in the street."

The angry woman yanks open one of the doors to a crib at the rear of the saloon and turns to stare past her shoulder. Leaned on the bar top, Everett still holds his same position, and the sunlit silhouette of Adeline remains standing in the saloon's front entrance. In a huff, Charlotte sneers toward them both, then spits to the floor with a curse in Spanish and slams the crib door closed behind her.

Chapter 21

The afternoon sun has dropped behind the higher structures of town, and the long shadows merge with another. Adeline steps down from the plank boardwalk into the dirt alleyway and walks around to the near side of the saloon. Leaned against the panel wall opposite, Hollister Tuckburrow stands waiting for her. Above his untrimmed facial hair, hollow eyes look up at the attractive young female. He lets his stern gaze and hard features soften as he speaks her name. "Hello Addie." He studies her with a reminiscent fondness, as she gradually strolls nearer. "How'd you ever find me?"

Adeline attempts to contain her beaming excitement, as she shrugs modestly and smiles at Tuck. "It sure wasn't easy."

They stand before each other in the alleyway, in silent contentment, until Tuck sniffs distracted and combs his fingers through his beard. "You can't stay around here."

"Then you can come back with me."

"I don't think so." Tuck looks away from her, tilting his head back on the wall of the wood building behind them. "Back to where?" He rocks his head and nearly closes his eyes. "That sort of life for me has been long gone... I can't return, and you can't stay here."

Adeline moves a few steps closer to the older man and feels the urge to reach out to him, but she restrains herself. "That life doesn't have to be gone. All can be right again."

Tuck thumps his head against the plank wallboard and stares off down the alley. His tightened mouth disappears into his tangle of beard whiskers as he chews on his lower lip. Emotions and remembered thoughts of their shared past begin to tug at Adeline's clenched jawline. Her chin trembles as she speaks, "I know it'll be okay if you come back..."

Tuck pushes away from the wall, standing to face her. "You need to leave this forsaken town and forget about me. Jest let that old life die and the past be done and gone."

Adeline musters her strength to hide powerful feelings. "If you come back with me ... I think we could start over." Her eyes glisten with tears, but she keeps her outward poise. "Come back with me. They aren't looking for you anymore."

He gazes down at her dusty boots, and finally looks up again to stare at the figure of a woman standing before him. "Take a good long look at me, Addie. Do I appear to be anything of that same person you once knew from back east? Tuck pushes away from the building and steps up to Adeline. He studies her as he attempts to move past, but then pauses. "I can't ever go back to that life." The outward appearance of the saloonkeeper suddenly turns ugly with a hard-edge tone. "I have no desire to be with those sorts of people ever again. Can't you understand that?"

A spiteful and angry sentiment begins to burn in Tuck's eyes, as he glowers at the innocent young woman before him. "I've been dead to those particular folks a good long time. What'll it take for you to see that? That life we knew is gone."
The restrained quiver of her chin resumes as she softly speaks. "Are all your feelings for me gone as well?"

Tuck meets her longing regard with a disgruntled scowl and abruptly turns away from her. "My dear... *Everything* you once knew of me is gone." Watching Tuck depart, Adeline holds back her tears.

At the mouth of the alley, Tuck halts at the main street. He returns his gaze to the alley and speaks over his shoulder, not having the courage to turn and engage with her again. "Go home, Adeline." His shoulders sag as he tilts his head. "You don't belong here in this world any more than I belong there in yours." Tuck walks out onto the street and, without a backward glance, turns round the corner of the saloon

Alone in the waning light, Adeline flutters her eyes. She swipes the back of her hand across her moistened cheek and peers out at the apparent emptiness of the border town. The fading sound of footsteps on the hard-packed dirt ends with the scrape of boot soles on the steps to the Barrelhouse.

~*~

In the shining moonlight, a solitary figure sits in the middle of the burned-out remnants of the old saloon building. The glowing shimmer of a filled whiskey bottle reflects off the lamplight from the relocated establishment down the street. Swirling the dark, intoxicating contents, the glass vessel is lifted high for another extended swallow.

The shadowed figure of Tuck sits propped on a stool in the charred remains, as his eyes glimmer with an orange glow from the distant porch lamps. His fiery gaze holds on the wavering lights, as he takes another pull at the liquor bottle and swipes his rolled up shirtsleeve across his bearded mouth. A low rumbling growl begins to boil up from deep inside, and Tuck takes the last drink of whiskey to finish off the bottle. "Dutch, you sanctimonious bastard... I have been exiled by yer kind before and will have no more of it."

Fingerlike wisps of clouds pass over the shining moon and Tuck's features fade into the shadows. He gazes out into the dusky street with a whiskey-fueled intensity growing inside him. The sounds of laughter echo from the busy saloon, and Tuck smashes the bottle against the burnt mess of ruins.

The drunken saloon owner kicks aside the scorched stool he was perched on and steps from the desolate ashes. Standing in the street, Tuck instinctively sweeps back his coat and touches his hand to the firearm holstered high on his hip. In an intoxicated haze, Tuck marches through town toward the lit porch of the renowned drinking establishment.

Chapter 22

The interior of Tuck's Barrelhouse maintains a boisterous atmosphere with people eating, drinking and playing cards. The glowing oil lamps burn warm and bright with a serene air of contentment all around. Seated across from his brother, Everett drinks at a table with Vic, where they have plates of food before them. Various saloon patrons sit or stand, drinking and smoking around the crowded room.

Everyone's attention turns at the sound of heavy boots pounding up the front stoop and the doors being kicked open. They all stare as they witness the saloon's drunken proprietor forcefully marching through the double-wide front doorway. Tuck proceeds to stagger to the bar and reaches over the slab to obtain a fresh bottle of whiskey. From behind the bar, Marlow moves over cautiously to his employer and whispers, "Are you okay boss?"

Tuck grabs the liquor bottle by the neck and shoves the bartender away to the back shelf of glasses. "Let me alone..."

At the back of the room, Charlotte moves from her place, entertaining customers, and swishes toward her suitor. "Are you upset, my sweet? You want me to get her gone?"

Tuck yanks the cork from the bottle and glowers at Charlotte in response to the blatant comment about Adeline. He reaches out at the sporting gal, violently grabs a fistful of red hair along the side of her head and snarls heartlessly. "Why don't you piss off and leave me the hell alone already! Go back to El Sueco where I found you..."

The flame-haired woman squirms awkwardly under his cruel grip, but she still tries to move closer to embrace him. "Come with me, Tuck. We can finally go and marry there."

"Get away from me." Tuck tugs her by the scalp and swings her toward the front doors. She stumbles and falls to her knees, as Tuck's violent deed discharges her on the floor. "Go on and git, I said!"

From the floor, Charlotte peers up at Tuck, broken-hearted, with tears glistening in her eyes. "You don't mean it."

Tuck takes another gulp from the liquor bottle and spits the mouthful on the floor at Charlotte. "Get out I said... And don't you ever come back!"

The woman wipes the mist of splashed whiskey from her face as she cowers on the floor, but doesn't move to exit. Tuck takes another pull from the fresh bottle and swings his booted foot back like he might actually kick her. The wooden legs of a chair rattle on the floorboards, scooting back from a table, and Everett calls across the room. "Hold it there, Tuck! There is no need for that."

Tuck spins and focuses his intoxicated glare at Everett. "You sonofabitch! Why didn't you tell me she was here?"

"I didn't think it would be your undoing."

Tuck remorsefully looks at the whiskey bottle in hand and then up at Everett again. An expression of troubled pain and sorrow comes through his harsh drunken countenance. "She doesn't belong here in this town. She can't stay."

Standing, Everett moves away from his chair and steps around the table. "Seems to be able to handle herself okay."

"What the hell do you know about it?"

Tuck puts the full jug to his lips and tips it upward. Rivulets of whiskey dribble through his chin whiskers and down his shirt and vest front, until he finally lowers the bottle. He stares blankly across the room, out the doors and then sways his head as if in a heated argument with only himself. "In the East, she knew a very different person years ago." Tuck lowers his chin as if recalling some sacred remembrance. "I had a civil life there, 'til they run me out... Not anymore!"

In the center of the saloon, Everett faces off with Tuck, who steadies himself against the bar. The town marshal glances at Charlotte on the floor, hunched on her knees, and moves slowly toward Tuck as if approaching a wild animal. "She may see it different."

Tuck stares at Everett with a fervently pained grimace. "She's a *woman...*"

Vic prepares to back his brother's play, as he stands up from his seat at the table, sweeps back his coat and speaks. "And from the looks of it... a mighty fine one at that."

Enraged, Tuck takes his gaze from Everett to Vic and growls angrily, "What does she know?"

Everett moves a step closer and speaks to Tuck in a calm, measured tone. "She a woman, who knows her mind."

Tuck rakes his fingers through his whiskey-soaked beard and lets out a despairing moan. "Get away from me... All of you!"

Kicking the toe of his boot out in a threatening gesture to Charlotte, Tuck jerks his pistol out with his free hand and waves it around the saloon. "Where are those damn Werners? I will kill 'em all tonight and be done with this devil dance."

Everett holds his ground midway across the saloon floor and lets his gun-hand sweep back over the butt of his holstered sidearm. "Put it away, Tuck."

The saloon owner spins and directs the aim of his cocked pistol at Everett and then at Vic. "I'll just as soon shoot you both for being in my damn way." Swaying a bit at the bar, Tuck jabs the gun upright and fires off a round into the air. "Just let me at them, and things will be done and square for you in this town. That's what you want anyway, isn't it?"

Everett advances slowly on Tuck, crowding his space. "That's not how it's going to be done."

"You're not a damned lawman, you selfish bastard!" Tuck sneers at Everett and looks around his shoulder to Vic. "All you and these brothers are is badge-wearing vigilantes who jest want to kill 'em yerself." He wags the discharged barrel of his pistol at the pair of lawmen while he shakes his head in disgust. "I ain't gonna wait anymore for you to do it." Drunkenly, the saloon owner raises and points his gun at a cowhand seated at a gaming table near the back of the room. "You there, where's your master?"

Tuck thumbs back the six-gun's hammer with a series of distinctive clicks. "Where is that dammed, cattle rustling, back-shooting, Werner trash when there's a fight to be had?" Tuck pulls the trigger, firing a gunshot that smacks high into the papered wall, missing inches above the cowboy's head. Chairs rattle across the floor and feet scuffle as everybody in the room scrambles for cover. Tuck snickers aloud as he cocks back the hammer on the pistol again.

With a few quick steps, Everett lunges forward and grabs Tuck's arm, pushing it downward as the gun fires into the floorboards. Everett twists the firearm from the saloon owner's grip and punches his clenched fist across Tuck's jaw. The fiery rage in Tuck's eyes fades to darkness, as he slumps to the dusty wood-plank floor.

Everett releases his hold on the drunken offender, and Tuck sprawls out in an unconscious daze alongside the bar. The room is in a hushed silence, as Everett glances up and around at the gathering bystanders. He nods to his brother, Vic, and waves Marlow over to the quiet figure on the floor. "Put him to bed and let 'em sleep it off." Everett sets Tuck's fired pistol on the bar-slab and steps around the laid out body. "And don't give 'im his gun back until he sobers up."

With a soft thump, the bottle releases from Tuck's grip. The dark whiskey in the glass vessel swishes and pours a wet path as it slowly rolls away from Tuck's hand, across the floor. Charlotte takes up the spilling container and climbs from her kneeling position. She steps forward and defiantly pushes out her ample bosom as she slams the whiskey bottle on the bar. "He'll kill you for what you done, Marshal."

Annoyed, Everett turns to her and shakes his head. "Oh, shut up!" He pulls his coat over his still holstered sidearm and marches toward the wide-open front entry doors. As Vic and Marlow gather Tuck's limp body from the floor, Everett stops at the threshold and turns back to the barroom. In a black-powder haze of lamplight, all eyes are on him.

Partly shadowed by the darkness outside, Everett lets his gaze travel around the occupants of the saloon interior. He speaks to those in the room with a steady and firm tone. "This doesn't change anything for those who are guilty from the Werner bunch... Next time, I'll let him kill them all." Everett turns to the dark street outside, descends the stairs from the boardwalk and fades into the shadowy night.

Chapter 23

The nameless Texas border town remains idle and quiet at the dawning of a new day. In the bright morning sunlight, Everett appears in the jail office doorway and steps outside. He remains on the shaded porch and narrows his gaze to the uninhabited length of street. At the far end of the settlement, he notices the livery man hitching up the horse and buggy for the town's female visitor.

Stepping out from behind, Ben walks onto the dusty, boardwalk and stops to observe the street alongside Everett. The older sibling glances slightly over at his brother and then continues his searching gaze. They both stand silently watching the working livery keeper at the far end of town, until the younger brother speaks the thoughts on his mind. "What good are we to do today, brother?"

Everett glances at Ben and then turns his gaze inside to the occupied jail cell toward the rear of the marshal's office. "They will come for him sooner or later." Everett smoothes his moustache whiskers aside and sighs, "This town has been at a low simmer for a long time now, and things will start to boil."

Ben rests his open hand on the walnut handle of the gun at his hip. "Vic and I were thinking to ride out and search for that canyon where they're hiding away our beeves." Everett nods. "Okay... Go on without me."

Ben looks inside the jail building and leans over to whisper low to Everett. "Vic was talking to Curtis before and thinks he might figure the spot they're using."

Everett nods his head again, but he continues his observation of the livery activity at the far end of town. "Alright, fine."

Ben spits into the street over the hitching rail and seems a bit disappointed by his sibling's lack of interest in regaining their stolen property. He watches Everett's attention on the horse and wagon as it is guided down the street to the hotel. "Don't you even care about what they took from us?"

Diverting his focus from the movement in the street, Everett looks aside at his little brother. "I care that they killed one of ours and will be sure that they answer for the deed." He looks back to the hotel and watches the front entrance. "After that, I'll worry about a stolen herd of dumb animals."

Ben nods and takes notice of Everett's keen interest in the horse drawn carriage across the street, as they both watch an attractive female figure appear at the doorway to the hotel. Everett stares quietly and Ben shakes his head and grunts, "You're the one looking to be the dumb animal."

"Yeah…" Everett lowers his chin, keeps his eyes forward and steps down from the boardwalk into the street. He strides across the dirt thoroughfare toward the four-wheeled carriage fronting the hotel. From the wide porch, Adeline descends the stairs, carrying her two bags of luggage which she sets down near the rear wheel of the buggy.

Everett steps over and lifts the bags from the ground, as she thanks the livery owner for his service. The lady turns to the lawman and raises an eyebrow at his unexpected arrival. "Are you here to escort me out of town?" Everett stands in the street with her bags and looks from the carriage to the hotel.

"Actually, I was thinking quite the opposite. I was going to ask you to stay awhile."

He walks over to the side of the street and sets the bags by the porch post on the boardwalk. Adeline moves away from the hind wheel of the wagon and stands near Everett. "He surely doesn't want me here. Yesterday he made it painfully clear that I should leave and forget all about him." Everett puts a hand out to hold on the porch support post, glances down the street to the saloon and back at Adeline. "He's not the one to say who can and can't stay in town."

Adeline lets a small smile form on her lips and tilts her head jauntily at the lawman. "But you can?" Everett pulls his coat back to reveal the law badge pinned on his vest and grins.

The lady traveler turns to the town and looks from the jail office to the old Spanish mission not far down the street. "That's a fine old ruin of a church."

Everett looks to the unused church, with its bell tower, situated near the center of the other abandoned buildings. "There are a lot of fine, neglected remnants around this town."

Adeline turns from the main street and puts her gaze upon her luggage placed on the hotel boardwalk. She offers up a bent arm toward Everett and smiles. "I'd be honored, Marshal, if you would escort me there and give me a tour."

A flush of color rises up from Everett's fastened shirt collar as he looks at the old mission church down the street. "Uhm… I didn't mean that exactly."

The adamant woman remains unmoved in the street with her arm offered up. Adeline peers over at Everett, with a devilish expression as she puts the badge-wearing lawman on the spot. "You are a gentleman, are you not?"

The lawman looks to the church uncomfortably and then at the woman waiting for him. "Hell… I haven't steered to one of them since I was a kid in short pants."

Everett moves from the hotel and takes her arm as she retorts, "You're never too far gone to find a little religion."

The two walk arm in arm down the wide empty street toward the abandoned mission building with the bell tower. As they pass near the front of the marshal's office, Ben stands in the shadowed doorway with Vic positioned close behind. Everett glances slightly over at the observing pair and turns forward again, as he escorts the lady down the street.

Inside the office doorway, Vic lets out a low, horse-like whinny which turns Ben's head to peer in over his shoulder. The older brother grunts, "I hope Tuckburrow is still cold."

Ben exchanges a roll of eyes with Vic and looks away. "Sure hope our brother don't lose himself to no fit of romance 'cause that's my department."

Vic nods his agreement and gazes out to the street from the interior shadows. "Can count on Everett to always do the thing he's good at... The pursuit of love ain't one of 'em."

Chapter 24

The adobe mission church appears to be a ruin in a steady state of disrepair, despite being framed by cloudless blue sky. Dry cracks spider-web the aged plaster walls, and white-washed sections of the exterior have fallen off to reveal the inner sunbaked mud-brick construction. Unhinging the yard gate to gain entry to the property, Everett escorts Adeline through the broken down fencing that surrounds the grounds. He gingerly places the section of unpainted pickets aside and escorts her to the large, wooden entry doors.

Everett gazes up at the old Spanish church admiringly. "As rundown as it is, there probably isn't a nicer thing in this out-of-the-way border town."

Adeline looks high to the crumbling, adobe bell tower. "There is no one to care for it?"

The lawman shakes his head and glances around at the overgrown yard and general neglect of the mission grounds. "It seems this whole town has been on hard times since the Holy Spirit was run out."

Adeline turns her attention to the lawman a moment and then gazes out to the rest of the mostly uninhibited buildings. "Such as, not having a name for the town?"

Everett looks from the tall, crumbling church walls down to the attractive-looking woman standing beside him. "Yes, that would be one of 'em."

"What's happening to this town, Everett?"

"A progress of sorts..." The marshal pauses as he realizes she has used his first name in a warm, sincere way. He seems to yearn for her to use it again and tries to find the right words to describe the town's complicated situation. "One man has had a tight collar on this place for too long." Everett looks over at Adeline and then back up at the mission church towering before them. "He's lost touch with what a thriving town needs, and mostly for what is right or wrong."

Adeline pushes open the tall, wooden entry doors and turns from the lawman to the interior of the abandoned church structure. "And you're going to show them the way?"

Everett stares inside the vacant building and exhales. "I'm here to right one wrongdoing. Then I'm going to leave it to the people here who care about having a life in this place."

She steps into the dark chapel and looks around at the decaying walls and ceiling. "Maybe the people who are still around need your guidance to help care for this place first." He lets his gaze wander to a holy cross on the neglected alter. "I buried one family member because of this town and don't plan to leave behind anymore."

The somber mood is suddenly broken by the soft chirps of a bird as it takes flight across the upper part of the chapel. It flutters up to the vaulted ceiling and out through a hole in the roof. Adeline takes another step inside and stands riveted, as she watches the dust linger in the air along shafts of light coming through broken windows and an unrepaired roof.

An empty, wooden cross hung on the wall attracts her attention and she speaks with a soft, quiet earnestness. "Everett... Sometimes discovering what you've been looking for doesn't give you the satisfaction you might anticipate." Her eyes study the timber cross and its crude construction. "You think mending that wrong or trying to put things back the way you think they ought to be will make it right again?" She reaches out to take hold of the lawman's available hand and draws him further into the deserted house of religion. "The fact is, sometimes it leaves you with an empty feeling you can't ever seem to fill."

Everett looks down at his hand entwined with hers. Standing in the quiet church chapel with a woman at his side, a sense of peace comes over him as he softens to her warmth. "He was a good man who was loved and deserved better."

Adeline looks away from the lawman and utters a response in the direction of the wooden cross. "Yes, he was."

They each individually reflect on their recent losses as bright streams of sunlight filter through the holy structure. She releases her hold on his hand and walks down the aisle. "Why don't we all leave this town and let it be what it is?" Everett stands, unmoved, witnessing her path to the altar, as she coyly glances over her shoulder at him and continues, "After we've gone, let the ones who care help it to progress."

Everett looks away from Adeline to a shiny piece of mirrored glass hung along the wall. In the cracked reflection, he studies the attractive woman's profile and then his own image behind with the star-shape marshal badge pinned on his vest. "I have a job to do." He gives her a slight tip of his hat brim and turns to walk out from the abandoned sanctuary.

At the entrance, Everett hesitates then turns to look at Adeline who stands illuminated by the beaming sunlight. "Good day to you, Miss Sonnett. I hope you choose to bless us with your presence in this no-name town awhile longer."

Adeline is silent as Everett steps outside, beyond the church doorway. After a short time, she carefully adjusts the skirting of her dress and takes another fleeting look around the abandoned sanctuary while murmuring, "I came here for something and I'm in no hurry to leave."

~*~

Two horseback figures ride through the long canyon-creased recesses of the terrain, well below the horizon line. Halting his mount, the rider in the lead studies the multiple trails of hooved livestock tracks scattered across the ground. Ben looks at Vic coming up behind and waves affirmative. "This is where they brought them through."

Vic looks skyward to a hawk floating on an updraft. "How long since they have been here, brother?"

Ben turns the head of his horse and trots over to the edge of the brushy trail. "A few days, maybe less."

Vic sits back in the saddle and scans his eyes around the cavernous trench in the landscape. He lifts his canteen from over his saddle horn, and the sharp snap of a gunshot rings out from the bushes ahead.

The open canteen drops to the sandy path and water gurgles out freely, as Vic slumps backward over the cantle. Ahead on the trail, a puff of powder smoke rises in the sky. Ben instantly puts spurs to his mount and races over to Vic, catching him in the stirrups before he tumbles out.

"Hold on there, Vic!"

"I'm a' holding the best I can..."

As the entangled horses circle each other in a fright, Ben draws his pistol and points in the direction of the ambush. He thumbs back the hammer and fires several rounds into the bushes while steadying Vic in the saddle seat. Taking the reins of his wounded brother's mount, Ben gives them a tug and urges his horse out of the ravine in the direction they came.

Ben leads Vic's horse at a nervous trot through the narrow terrain. He fires another shot into the concealing brush before urging the fleeing horses to a loping gallop. Suffering, Vic hunches over the saddle horn and lets out a wounded moan as they race away from the trail of the stolen cattle.

Chapter 25

The dentist's office sits at the west end of town just across the way from the livery barn. Everett marches down the vacant street through the middle of town, leaps the steps up to the porch and gives a short knock on the window-paneled door. "It's Everett... How is he?" He pushes the office door open and lets it swing aside.

Laid down across the mealtime table in the front office, Vic has a fresh bandage around his middle with a hint of rosy coloring showing through at the side of the bullet wound. Stepping inside, Everett looks at Ben, who is guarding at the window with a rifle. He swings the door shut and speaks to the doctor. "How is he Doc?"

"With a bit of rest and healing, he'll probably survive." The doctor stands working over a blood-tinged wash basin, cleaning and putting away his operating tools as he talks. "The bullet only grazed and bounced off a rib, tearing away some flesh and bruising the area on his chest. It looked to be a nasty wound at first but will heal fine if properly cared for."

Everett pushes aside the curtain on the door and peeks out the glass panes before he moves to Ben at the window. "What happened out there?"

The youngest brother seems distrustful of the doctor hearing and motions Everett nearer. "We had just got the trail of them stashed beeves when we were bushwhacked."

"Any idea who done it?"

Ben holds his rifle with the barrel pointed upward at the ceiling and looks out the doctor's office window toward the livery across the street. "I have a real good idea who."

Propping himself on an elbow, a groan escapes as Vic rouses. He winces at the painful area under the bandage on his chest. "We don't know 'xactly who done the shootin' so don't go makin' it worse by castin' aspersions."

Ben shakes his head, miffed at his eldest brother, and glances shrewdly at Everett. "If it warn't the Werners, then who was it?"

The wounded brother eases back down on the work table with a grunt and turns his head to the waiting doctor. "Doc, hand me that medicinal whiskey jug again, will ya?" The doctor passes over the remains of a bottle, and Vic props himself up just enough to get a good mouthful. He wipes the damp dribble from his chin and turns his attention to Everett. "There might be some good boys yet in that cattle outfit, and we cain't go to murderin' them all." The doc's eyes go wide at the mention of prospective killings.

Everett affirms with a nod and eases aside the window curtain to stare down the street to the saloon and then the jail. "I thought we had the worst of 'em locked up already."

Holding the rifle at his chest, Ben grumbles grudgingly. "If you ride for that brand, then you're a part of the problem. Rustlin' cattle and shooting down men from ambush is what they seem to do, so they're all one 'n the same in my book."

Everett considers his hot-headed, younger brother's opinion and motions to the jailhouse. "Ben, head over and keep watch on our prisoner, after you see to it that Vic gets what he needs. I'm gonna have a talk with Tuckburrow."

Ben cradles the rifle across his arm and watches out the window to the Barrelhouse saloon as he responds to Everett. "It may turn out that he's been no better than the rest of 'em." The door swings open and closes behind as Everett exits. From inside, Ben watches as his brother steps off the porch and makes his way down the street toward Tuck's saloon.

~*~

The town is its usual quiet as Everett marches down the long stretch of dusty street, with his keen attention focused on the dull panes of overlooking windows. Nearing the saloon building, he passes the alley between structures and hears a familiar-accented female voice speak out from the concealing shadows. "Is he dead yet?"

The heartless tone of the inquiry turns Everett on his heel to recognize Charlotte standing with a cigarette in hand. He stops short, stares at her while she takes another inhaling drag and then walks to her. "What do you know about it?"

"I know you are all soon to be dead men."

A flush of anger begins to rise in Everett, as he climbs the stairway to meet her. "You know the ones who did it?"

Everett is momentarily distracted when he sees Adeline exit the hotel and walk the boardwalk toward the saloon. Charlotte notices his diverted attentions and leans forward around the corner of the building to take a look for herself. She gives a pouty huff when she sees her perceived nemesis. "Why is she still here?"

Adeline walks along the front of the buildings and hesitates in front of the double doors to the barrelhouse. Charlotte steps from the alleyway, near Everett and calls out. "Go 'n get away from here, girl. Tuck does not want you!"

Everett forcefully shoves the fiery redhead backward, trying to restrain her. "She is none of your business."

"Tuck is my man and what he wants *is* my business!"

Adeline hesitates at the saloon entry and then decides to approach Everett and Charlotte. She steps up to the pair at the alleyway and addresses the angry woman glaring at her. "I will leave this town when I'm ready and choose to do so..." She gives Everett a look, "Or when I am escorted out."

Charlotte tosses her rolled cigarette away and sneers. "There will be no more lawman to protect you very soon. They already shot one of his damn brothers."

Adeline looks to the marshal with concern, and he lowers his head slightly while turning a stern eye to Charlotte. "You know who done it?"

The saloon entertainer curls her upper lip and snarls. "It doesn't matter, as you all have it coming."

Adeline reluctantly watches as Everett forcefully blockades Charlotte in the alleyway. The lawman pushes her to the wall of the adjacent building and speaks harshly at her. "Miss, you are a vicious and ugly person."

Charlotte looks over Everett's shoulder and flashes a wicked grin to Adeline. "If I had my way, I'd tell those Werner boys to finish their task with you at the stagecoach."

A sense of unease crosses Adeline's features, and she turns to walk away. Everett is unexpectedly shoved aside, as Charlotte lunges past him and tackles Adeline to the ground. The two women tumble from the boardwalk and hit the dirt in a whirling flutter of upturned skirts and twisting bodices. Rolling and thrashing with each other, the fight is a vicious flurry of slaps, screams and hair pulling.

A crowd of saloon customers instantly flood from the double doors and fan out across the boardwalk to watch the entangled females battle it out. Everett leaps to the street and tries to grab hold of one of the combatants. "That's enough!" A ladies foot kicks out, and Everett jumps back to avoid a sweeping blow. Finally, he grabs a fleeting handful of fiery red hair and gives it a firm tug. Charlotte wails and shrieks like a roped wildcat, as the lawman pulls her from the bout.

Along to Presidio

From behind, Everett secures a firm hold around Charlotte's middle, as she kicks and screams obscenities in Spanish toward Adeline and every observer along the street. Standing by and dusting herself off, Adeline takes a step toward Charlotte, who wriggles violently in Everett's arms. Adeline regains her winded breath as she considers how to appropriately address her accoster.

Giving her an additional squeeze, Everett holds Charlotte tight, which makes her struggle and squirm more. She screams out, as she tries to wrestle her arms loose and scratch her way to freedom. "Tuck will kill you this time!" Everett manages to hold her arms secure and keep her from clawing as she shrieks, "You are a dead man, and he will kill you and the rest of your family!"

He lowers his mouth to her ear. "Did he tell you that?"

"He lets no man burden him! He'll kill you all!"

Adeline stands in the street before Everett and Charlotte and speaks out with a near frantic tone of voice. "Stop talking about Hollister! He's not that kind of man."

Charlotte snarls at Adeline, nearly frothing from the mouth. "You should go back to where you came from."

Adeline flushes with an intense abhorrence and takes a step toward the fitfully restrained woman. Suddenly, she reels her balled hand back and swings at Charlotte's jaw.

The redheaded woman takes the blow directly across her chin and slumps to the side. Everett holds the sagging form of Charlotte in his arms and stares, aghast, at Adeline massaging a clenched fist. "Miss... That was quite the punch."

Adeline stares at the partly-conscious woman a moment and then marches up the steps to the Barrelhouse. She pushes the bystanders aside, as they mutter aloud while dispersing back into the saloon.

Chapter 26

Standing in the street with Charlotte in his arms, Everett grudgingly hoists her collapsed body over his shoulder and proceeds to walk toward the jailhouse. He nearly makes it to the steps of the marshal's office, when three horseback cowboys come around the corner, with Jenks riding in front. The burdened lawman heaves a labored breath and pushes a ruffle of skirt aside from his face, as the cowboys position their mounts around him in a semi-circle.

Jenks leans down on the saddle horn, stares at the lawman, then looks aside at his men and spits to the street. "Hey Marshal, did you have to pay extra to shut her up?" Everett turns slowly and adjusts the semi-conscious body on his shoulder, as she moans feebly. Amused, the horseback assembly snickers as Jenks continues. "Is it okay if we treat the woman-folk as you do? Or, do we need a badge for that?"

Deliberately evaluating the odds, Everett sweeps back his coat tail to reveal the holstered firearm perched at his hip. A gusting breeze flutters the woman's skirting across Everett's face, and he calmly pushes it down to her rump. With hard, steely gazes, the lawman and ranch foreman stare at each other across the distance, despite the ruffled distraction. Everything else seems to fade away, as the two men decide if they will take this opportunity to try to kill each other.

Ben steps out from the marshal's office doorway and stands on the porch with a short-barreled shotgun in hand. "Hello there, brother. You need a hand with some of that?" Everett continues the face-off with Jenks and the cowboys, as they start backing down under the leveled aim of Ben's sawed-off scattergun. The blockade of riders begins to loosen and drift, as their horses are eased backward.

Eyeing Ben on the porch stoop, Jenks and the others seem to lose interest with the new addition to the showdown. Weighing the changed odds, which no longer look favorable, Jenks waves the cowboys across the street to the Barrelhouse. "C'mon boys, let it be." He spits aside and grumbles low. "That short-horn has a bit too much greenness in his belly to be standing 'hind a street howitzer."

Ben puts the side-by-side to his shoulder and points the barrels directly at Jenks. "That's right. Y'all best be gettin'." The young deputy cocks the hammer on the second barrel. "You ever seen the kind of oozing corpse this sort of thing leaves at a short distance?" He narrows an eye and smirks. "Care to find out?"

Jenks glares at the shotgun-wielding deputy on the jailhouse porch and then returns to focus attention on Everett standing with them in the street. "We'll surely see ya again." He looks to the rump of the woman draped over the lawman's shoulder and shrugs. "Nice talkin' with ya, loverboy."

Everett continues to stare them down as they turn their horses to move away. After the cowboys reach the other side of the street, Everett turns to look at his brother on the porch. Ben reluctantly lowers the shotgun, as the Werner cowboys dismount and tie their horses in front of the Barrelhouse. Everett readjusts the weight of the woman over his shoulder and steps up to the boardwalk. "Thanks, little brother."

Ben cradles the shotgun over his forearm and leans on the office doorframe. "I was going to let ya go a bit longer." He uncocks the hammers on the scattergun and continues, "Wasn't sure on your draw under that pile of petticoats."

Everett steps to the porch and moves past Ben through the door of the jailhouse. "I wasn't too sure on it myself."

~*~

In the rear quarters of the marshal's office, Everett puts Charlotte down on one of the unused cell bunks. He steps back to swing the jail door closed to a solid *thunk* of iron bars. Ben stands inside the partitioning doorway, holding the short-barreled shotgun. He gazes from the cell occupied by Curtis to the other holding Charlotte. "You gonna lock the door?"

Everett steps past the other cells and shakes his head. "We don't want her in here any longer than really needed."

Curtis stands inside his confined cage, looks over at the other cell and leans his hands through the set of bars. "What'd she do to git knocked around and put in here?" Everett continues his course to the front part of the office, ignoring the remarks of the previous detainee. The locked-up cowboy stares after him and then looks to Ben at the doorway. "How about you, deputy? You have a thing to say in what goes on 'round here?"

With the cell bars between, Ben stands facing Curtis. "She ain't been restrained. Jest put up here to rest for a while. If you don't watch yer mouth, you'll be shut up the same."

Curtis ponders the threat and forces a sneering laugh. "You cain't harm me none or Dutch will skin yer hide." Walking to the jail cell, Ben stops, turns away, then suddenly whirls and slams the butt of the shotgun into the bars directly in front of Curtis, jolting him backward onto the jail bunk. Angry and embarrassed, he glares out at the deputy and spits, "You'll get yours yet, boy…"

Ben grins and follows after Everett to the front office. Seated behind the desk, Everett glances up at Ben and then back to the occupants of the cells. "He giving you problems?"

The younger brother snorts as he moves across the room to glimpse out the window. "Nope. I just had to put him in his place a bit." He places the shotgun behind the door and peers over at his brother. "Why'd you bring her in here?"

Everett adjusts the comfort of his holster rig along the seat, and with a creak, leans the chair against the wall. "Appears Tuckburrow's various womenfolk don't seem to get along with one another." Ben looks out the front window across the street to the hotel and then over toward the saloon. Everett puts a boot to the edge of the desktop and continues, "Must have a glass-jaw, 'cause that gal jest poked her once." With a grin, Ben looks over at Everett. "You sayin' that new filly in town knocked out that red-maned wildcat?"

"Yep."

"That fine-looking thing really done that?"

"Might've been a lucky jab... Might not."

Ben swings the gun-port shutter closed on the window and leans a shoulder against the adobe brick wall. He looks at the unsecured jail cell with Charlotte lain out on the bunk. "Any gal that can handle herself like that is fine in my book." The deputy peers back outside to the saloon across the street. "You find out about her relationship with Tuck?"

"Nope. They're a mite sensitive at the mention of it."

"Well, between you and me, brother, that pretty gal having anythin' to do with that crusty character seems odd." Everett nods in agreement and stands up from the desk chair. "Yes, it do..." The lawman adjusts his arm in his coat sleeve and walks to the front doorway. "I'm going to have a friendly word with Tuck." Everett stands next to Ben. "I'd like to hear if he has anything to say about that ambush on you and Vic."

"Want me to come along?"

Everett glances toward the rear-most lineup of jail cells. "You best stay here in case that hellcat comes around and gets any funny ideas." At the entryway to the marshal's office, Everett adjusts his hat and covers his coat over his holstered sidearm and law badge. He steps across the threshold and swipes a finger at his hat brim toward his younger brother before pulling the door closed behind. "See ya shortly."

Chapter 27

A whirlwind of dust swirls across Everett's path in the street as he approaches the front boardwalk of Tuck's Barrelhouse. Watching him walk up, a D/W cowhand waits on the porch. He is joined by Jenks and the other one at the front door, as Everett starts to climb the first step.

The lawman pauses on the steps and stares up at Jenks. The ranch foreman holds a newly purchased bottle of whiskey and stands in the doorway with a look of spiteful animosity. Everett lets his hand hang loose at his side, fingers spread, ready to sweep back his coat and draw his gun in an instant. "You have something to say to me, cowboy?"

Jenks smiles and lets one of the doors swing closed behind him. He looks to the cowboy behind on the porch, holding a fresh bottle, and steps to the middle of the walkway. "I really don't have much of anything to say to you, Marshal."

Everett draws back his coat to reveal the badge pinned on his vest then rests his open palm on his holstered gun. "You were awful lippy o'er yonder."

The lawman tilts his head across the street to the jail and, as if on cue, the two cowboys step up alongside Jenks. The foreman grins, sensing things have shifted in his favor. "Hear tell, you're gonna try 'n arrest us for puttin' yer kin in the ground?"

A heat rises up in Everett as he addresses the cowboys. "To which incident are you referring?"

Jenks grins, as he glances to his hired hands beside him. "It's jest a matter of time 'fore every one of you is put down like the dirty law-dogs you pretend to be. If'n we don't do it, Tuck will surely finish the job for us." Everett slowly takes on the remaining stairs, steps to the boardwalk and stands close-up in Jenk's face. "Are you the one to do it here and now?" The lawman stands firm, as he faces down the ranch foreman. In a snarling tone, Everett challenges Jenks. "Or, you gonna wait for a more opportune time to bushwhack us?"

The standoff on the saloon porch continues, unabated, while the cowboys at Jenks' flank ease back to make room. Down the street, the slam of a door is heard followed by the lever of a rifle, and Jenks momentarily lets his eyes flit away. Everett remains steadfast before them, as Jenks lets out a disappointed breath, "Damn you and your kinfolk…"

Down the street, at the door to the doctor's building, Vic stands bare-chested with a bandage around his middle and a rifle tucked at his shoulder. The targeted sights of the long gun are directly upon the pair at the front of the saloon. Jenks returns his gaze to Everett and sidesteps around him. "Aw, we was jest foolin' Marshal. No harm intended."

Everett takes a calming breath and keeps a stern eye on the three Werner cowboys across from him on the porch. "Jenks, you tend to be the fool too often."

Containing his ire, Jenks glances down the street to Vic with the rifle and steps around Everett to the tied horses. "Come on boys, grab them bottles." As he climbs onto his horse, the cowboys load their saddlebags and tighten cinches. Jenks nudges his mount forward toward the saloon porch stoop and leans down to speak in a quiet tone toward Everett. "We'll be sure to dance another day, when you don't have one of yer damned brothers backin' you up."

Nearly at the same level, Everett stares direct at Jenks. "I'll be waiting." With a sneer, Jenks turns his horse and gallops out of town with the two Werner cowboys in tow. Everett lets his gaze travel toward the doctor's office and watches Vic lower the rifle's aim. The injured man props himself against the door frame and gives a dismissive wave, as Everett returns the gesture with an affirming nod and turns to enter the Barrelhouse.

~*~

The three riders run their horses past the edge of town. Jenks chokes back the reins on his excited mount and wheels his horse around to face the cowboys following on his flank. He stares at one of the mounted cowboys and growls orders. "Coe, go 'n find Dutch!" His fidgety horse wants to keep moving and Jenks pulls its head around, causing his steed to spin as he talks. "Tell 'im the new marshal has got that whore he likes locked up with Curtis. If he wants to keep this town under control, he'll have to do some proper housecleaning."

The horse begins to crow-hop, and Jenks gives some slack on the reins as he lopes around the heeding cowboys. Jenks jabs a finger at the other cowhand and waves him on. "You and I will go head to the stock tanks and gather up the rest of the boys to meet at the ranch."

Coe sits his horse as it moves sideways from the skittering mount of the foreman. "You want me to tell 'im the part about killin' the marshal?"

"No gol-dammit!" Jenks glares at Coe and shakes his head with distain. "He best come up with that part on his own if he's going to keep swinging his weight around this town. Jest tell about the whore and ask his plans to get Curtis out." The cowboy nods and spurs his horse on toward the ranch. Jenks watches him ride over the hilltop to the horizon and looks back at the town before he turns to the other cowhand. "We got some guns to gather." Jenks and the remaining cowboy urge their agitated mounts to a lope, and they ride off in the other direction toward the rising terrain.

Chapter 28

The interior of Tuck's Barrelhouse has the usual middling crowd of out-of-work loafers, cowboys and pastime gamblers. Scanning his eyes among the somewhat familiar faces, Everett marches through the room and stops at the rear doors leading to the cribs in back. A long-in-the-tooth, wrinkled prostitute sits in a chair watching the barroom for prospective business. Everett addresses her, "Where's Tuck?"

She regards him with a slanted eye. "Who?"

He taps her chair with his boot toe and pulls back his coat to reveal the star-badge. The woman looks up through cracked makeup and grunts, "I already know who you are."

Everett retorts, "Then you know I mean business."

Raising her arm, she points at the door in the rear. Everett strides down the short hallway and pounds on the indicated door. "Hollister Tuckburrow?"

There is the sound of splashing water from a bathing tub inside, then silence. Everett raps his knuckles on the wooden door again, calling out, "Tuckburrow, you in there?"

There is a pause and then the muffled voice of Tuck is heard from the other side of the door. "Piss off, Marshal."

Everett lifts his leg and gives the door handle a kick. The wooden door slams open and Everett enters with his pistol in hand. A partially nude woman shrieks and lunges for something to cover up with as Tuck sits in the bathing tub. With soapy water up around his chest and pale suds hanging from the tip of his beard, the two men glare at each other. Tuck splashes some water to rinse his chin-whiskers and finally speaks. "You got somethin' to say, Marshal?"

Everett averts his eyes from the half-dressed woman cowering in the far corner and looks to Tuck settled in the tub. "I want to have a talk with you."

Seated low in the bath water, the saloon owner's eyes are level with the barrel of the gun. He stares at the loaded cylinder and looks up to the lawman. "Figured there was a good reason for disturbin' my wash.

Everett lowers the tip of his gun and gestures outside. "We need to speak out back."

Tuck shifts in the tub and rises from the cloudy bath. "You can say yer piece now, Marshal."

Everett matches Tuck's even stare, undistracted by him and his soaking-wet nudity, then turns to the broken door. "Come outside... I'll be waiting." Grabbing the busted handle, Everett glances over his shoulder at the topless woman in the corner and the conspicuously unclothed man in the bathtub. "And get some pants on."

Tuck remains standing as Everett swings the door shut behind him. He turns to his female bathing partner squatted in the corner and smiles. "Some friends sure can be quaint." He reaches into the soapy water with a scraping, clank against the tub bottom and scoops a pistol from the clouded depths. "Dry this off for me and reload it again, will you darlin'?"

The girl comes over with a small drying towel and Tuck hands over the dripping-wet handgun. She wraps up the pistol and Tuck pulls the bath towel from covering her torso. "Thank ya honey, there's no need to be shy in front of me." She clutches the bundled handgun to her chest and turns away as Tuck dries off, staring at the closed door before him.

Along to Presidio

From the backend of town, three galloping horsemen ride in front of the jail and skid their mounts to a sliding stop. A cloudy haze of dust rolls across the front boardwalk and Ben steps outside with the short-barreled scattergun in hand. He brings the street howitzer up level with his waistline and directs the double barrels of the shotgun toward the men horseback with bandanas covering a portion of their faces. "What do you fellers want?"

One of the cowboys squints across the distance and speaks through his pulled-up scarf. "Is the marshal in there?"

"He's out and about. How can I be of service to ya?"

The horseman positioned in the middle looks to the cowboy next to him and adjusts his neckerchief over his nose. The dust settles as they move into positon, fronting the jail. Despite the covering bandana, the lead's voice seems familiar. "I hear tell that you have a gal in there with Curtis?"

"That's right. She's just visitin'."

The rider settles his mount and stares hard at Ben. "You listen here, deputy-lawman… Dutch is the only one 'round here who people answer to." His narrowed gaze darts beside to the mounted riders on each flank and continues, "Folks are gonna git kilt if you keep pokin' the tiger."

Pulling back both hammers on the double-barreled shotgun, Ben keeps it pointed at the bandana-clad horsemen. "Folks have already been killed along with property stole."

"This is about a few cows?"

The afternoon sun glints off Ben's youthful features as he boldly faces off with the trio of veiled, mounted cowboys. "This is about doing justice for a man buried o'er yonder."

The lead rider sits straighter in the saddle and grunts, "Puttin' Dutch's boy in jail ain't gonna bring back yer kin."

Ben angles the double-barrels higher, to the man's face. "We aim to return the favor and punish those responsible with a short rope 'n a quick drop."

Above the covering bandana, the rider narrows his eyes as he pushes back his duster to expose his holstered sidearm. "If'n you ain't real careful with that ol' scattergun, Deputy, someone might git hurt."

Ben stands on the porch with the shotgun pointed at the three men on horseback and warily watches each of them. "Y'all can jest go on 'n git now. Unless you have a confession for us, you ain't needed here."

The lead cowboy fixes his fierce glare upon the deputy. A tense moment transpires between the horseback men and lone lawman. Ultimately, the foremost rider slowly raises his hand with the reins and jabs a pointed finger at the deputy. From beneath the pulled up bandana the cowboy growls, "This town is ours, ya hear… And Dutch Werner says yer no longer welcome in it!"

Chapter 29

In the alley behind the Barrelhouse, Everett stands with his back against the wall, waiting for Tuck to make his entrance. Gazing around, he has a restricted view of the empty street. The afternoon sun on the horizon begins to dip below the skyline of the town and cast the far reaches into shadow.

The rear exit door of the Barrelhouse saloon opens wide and Tuck unhurriedly steps out fully dressed. He descends the few steps and stands opposite the lawman in the alleyway. Everett moves from the alley wall, keeping his back to the sun, and waits as Tuck shifts to the middle, between the buildings. Both men let their arms dangle near their holstered sidearms, studying each other while the evening shadows push the remaining sunlight up the adjoining wall.

Facing west, Tuck squints into the last of the daylight. He waits patiently until the brightest rays wane, so he can make out the features of the lawman standing opposite him. "Before we go on 'n kill one another, what's this all about?"

Everett has both hands relaxed at his side but keeps his coat tail pulled back, ready to draw his firearm in an instant. "Did you tell folks around town you were aimin' to scrag us?"

Tuck squints from the sun behind Everett and wrinkles his brow inquisitively. "Who did you hear that from?"

"A red-headed birdie chirped around town."

"That whore... Charlotte?"

Everett offers a slight nod and Tuck grins, undisturbed. The saloon owner calmly reaches his hand upward to sweep the long moustache whiskers away from his parted lips. "Don't remember exactly, to tell the truth." He smirks smugly. "I say lots of things to appease her if it gets me what I want." Not to be misdirected by Tuck's primping, Everett keeps his focus on the hand near the gun as the saloon owner continues, "Could be... I probably did tell her I was to kill you."

"Now's your time."

As Everett stands ready, Tuck looks down at the long shadow on the ground and then back up at the town marshal. "I'd be happy to accommodate you sometime, but I'm not the one who murdered yer kin, if that's what yer gettin' at."

Everett shifts his stance but remains ready to draw. "Are you speaking of what happened today?"

Tuck lets his gaze fall to the lawman's shadow again and asks interestedly, "What about your business today has anything to do with mine?"

Everett studies Tuck's sun-drenched features in the waning light of day. "Vic was dry-gulched, but he's alive yet."

Tuck turns and glances down the side alleyway to the town street with its run-down mix of ramshackle buildings. "I'd say you're all men marked for death, but not by me." Tuck takes a step to Everett and reduces the glare of the sun. "Is that what's stuck in yer craw?" They both stand fixed in a tense deadlock, each ready to draw on the other.

~*~

At the front of the marshal's office, Ben holds his station with the shotgun directed at the set of masked riders. The sun drops nearer to the horizon, and the remaining rays of light glint off the glass windows of the town structures. With a snort, one of the saddled mounts impatiently stomps a foreleg to the ground.

Along to Presidio

Calmly, the cowboy on the right draws his sidearm, points the revolver and places his thumb over the hammer. Despite their faces being partly concealed by bandanas, the other cowboys' eyes turn up with eager smiles of approval. The rider positioned in the middle puts his hand firmly over the grip of his sidearm but keeps it holstered. "Listen here, law-pup, I've had 'bout enough of all this nonsense. Put up that scattergun, so no one gits hurt." He nods his head aside. "Step away now 'n let us git ol' Curtis outta there."

Ben wags his head to the contrary and redirects his aim to the horseman at the center. "Tell your man to put away that pistol or I'll cut 'im down right after I let a barrel go on you."

The veiled leader keeps his hand on the wooden grip of his holstered pistol and the tension of the standoff increases. From the rear jail cell of the lockup, a shouting voice calls out and catches everyone's attention in front. "You got 'im boys! He's alone! Shoot 'im already!"

Ben turns his head and hollers inside. "Quiet now!"

The mounted cowboy, with his gun pointed, cocks it and glances to the riders beside for guidance. The lead rider offers a slight nod, as he abruptly draws his own handgun. The cowboy lets go a gunshot that slams into Ben's shoulder, pushing him back against the jamb of the doorway.

Despite the shock of the bullet hit, Ben unleashes a barrel of the side-by-side shotgun into the man who shot him. The close range spread of pellets tear through the rider's head and torso as he erratically fires another shot from his pistol. Killed almost immediately, the buckshot victim reels over backward from the impact and flops to the ground in a heap.

The empty saddle-horse bolts and lunges sideways in the street as the drifting cloud of burnt gunpowder wafts by. The two remaining masked horseman have their sidearms drawn and cocked but are distracted by their skittish mounts.

Waving his revolver toward the jailhouse, the leader of the cowboys turns to the remaining rider and directs him inside. "Git in there and spring Curtis loose!"

The cowboy spins from the saddle stirrups with his pistol ready and jumps to the boardwalk. He dashes past the wounded deputy, who slowly slides down the door frame. The still-mounted cowboy adjusts the bandana over his face and looks to his fallen companion oozing blood into the dry, dirt street. He aims his pistol at Ben and yells to the deputy. "You done kilt 'im!"

Jockeying for a better positon behind the dismounted steed of the other rider, the lingering horseman jerks his mount backward from the porch as Ben unloads the other barrel of the shotgun at him. The injured deputy's buckshot goes astray and tears into the support post for the awning. The lone horseman stretches out his gun arm and fires off a shot at the slumped deputy, as his horse bucks into the street.

Ben receives a second slug of bullet lead to the thigh. Despite his injuries, he braces himself in the doorway while he breaks open the shotgun and ejects the empty brass casings. Bleeding from the gunshot wounds to his shoulder and hip, Ben digs into his pocket, bringing out a pair of shotgun loads. He drops them into the barrels of the side-by-side scattergun with a hollow *thunk* and snaps closed the breech.

The remaining rider gets control of his saddle mount and shouts at the wounded deputy collapsed on the porch. "You damned, stupid fool... It didn't have to go this way!" The horseback cowboy thumbs back the hammer on his pistol and fires another shot that smashes through the wood siding right beside Ben's head. He frantically spins his horse in the street and calls out to his man inside the marshal's office. "What the hell ya doin' in there? Git that boy sprung!"

Along to Presidio

Curtis appears at the doorway behind the slumped deputy and violently pushes his boot to Ben's shoulder, shoving him aside from the entrance. He steps out to the boardwalk and stands over the gunshot-wounded lawman. "You's just another corpse in the makin', like them others." The other bandana-wearing cowboy follows outside the office, and Curtis reaches around him to grab at his holstered pistol. "Give me that hogleg of yourn, and I'll put this one in the ground for good, too."

Curtis grabs at the cowboy's gun, and there is a short wrestle for the firearm until the cowboy finally gives it up and jumps to the street for his horse. The rancher's son stands above the wounded deputy sprawled on the boardwalk and calmly pulls back the hammer of the single-action revolver. Curtis grins as the loaded cylinder turns with a fateful click. "Say hello to yer dead kinfolk fer me..."

From a prone position, Ben quickly raises the loaded barrels of the shotgun and squeezes back one of the triggers. The deafening discharge from the close-range buckshot explodes into the target's midsection. The sudden impact spins Curtis against the building where he lingers a moment before falling to the boardwalk in a blood-spattered mess.

The disarmed cowboy leaps to the saddle of the nearest available horse and the mount circles as he grabs at the reins. The two horsemen look down at the shotgun-blasted cowboy in the street and the collapsed, bloody corpse of the rancher's son splayed out on the boardwalk. The rider calls out to Ben. "You'll pay for this ... We'll be back to kill you all!"

Ben winces at the splinters stuck to the side of his face from the bullet hit on the wall. He shoots the remaining barrel of the shotgun into the street and the lead pellets rake across the flank of the last, rider-less horse. The two surviving cowboys keep their bandanas held up and race out of town.

~*~

Still in a stalemate, Everett and Tuck hear the blasting gunshots coming from the main street. The marshal steals a glance to the alley and the observant saloon owner grimaces. "Yer sort of business, I assume? You better git to it, Marshal." Tuck peers down the side alley of the Barrelhouse as a riderless horse trots past in the street. "I ain't goin' anywheres."

Everett carefully moves his hand away from his holstered sidearm and lets his coat fall forward to cover over. He stares at Tuck and then jabs a finger at him as he turns. "Our business will have to wait. This affair ain't yet settled."

Tuck nods and steps to Everett. "I'll follow yer lead." The marshal turns and strides quickly down the alleyway and then jogs toward the source of the recent shots in the street.

At his heels, Tuck follows.

Chapter 30

The town is deathly still as Everett, accompanied by Tuck, steps from behind the saloon building. The smoky cloud of spent gunpowder lingers in the air, near the marshal's office. A gruesome scene is revealed with one body laid out near the hitching post and two others slumped on the boardwalk near the jailhouse doorway.

Everett draws his pistol and breaks into a trotting run as he calls out to his younger brother. "Ben... I'm coming!" The lawman quickly glimpses the buckshot-riddled remains of the bandana-shrouded cowboy flopped in the street and hops the boardwalk to the pair of bodies at the door entry. The leather soles of his boots skid to a stop next to his fallen brother and Everettt reaches down to cradle him in his arms. "Ben... Are you alive yet? I'm here."

The young deputy makes a valiant effort to look up at his older sibling and the pain from his injuries makes his face contort with agony. "I got myself shot up real good, brother." Everett holds Ben in his arms and looks over the bloody wounds on his upper body and leg. He takes a kerchief from his pocket and presses it to the bullet wound on his shoulder. "You're gonna be okay, little brother... Don't say anything. Just be still and we'll get that doctor."

Tuck nudges the limp body in the street over with the side of his boot and lowers the bandana covering the face.

Recognizing the cowboy, Tuck grimaces at the messy result of the scattered shotgun wound and speaks up to the porch. "Buckshot to the head and shoulders." Tuck turns his body to gaze down the main street at the loose horse still wandering. "This one won't be needin' a doctor."

Everett holds Ben tight in his arms to comfort him as Tuck steps up to the porch and studies the dead form of Curtis slumped against the wall. "Dutch is gonna be none too pleased to hear tell his son has been kilt. How 'bout him?"

Everett smoothes the sweat-matted hair back from Ben's forehead and looks up. "If you could get that doctor over here, I would be much obliged." The saloon owner peers down at the wounded deputy and nods solemnly.

~*~

The jail cells in back of the marshal's office are illuminated by a pair of turned-up lanterns, set close together. Vic, Everett and Tuck stand outside one of the barred cells as the doctor leans over Ben and finishes wrapping his wound. In the other lock-up, Charlotte appears morbidly curious as she hugs her knees to her chest on the bunk and peeks over. She gazes at Tuck and the pair of brothers outside the cell. "Y'all enjoying the action in town of late?"

Vic glances over and gives the barroom gal a stern look. "Lil' lady, you would be best advised to keep your trap shut, if you know what's good for you." Charlotte sneers at them, her eyes glimmering with the orange glow of the lantern light. "I ain't done anything wrong for you to be keepin' me here." She sits on the bunk and turns away as Tuck glares at her.

Tuck grumbles under his breath to the jailed female. "Except be a witness to Dutch's boy gettin' sprung 'n kilt."

Charlotte looks back to meet his stare with contempt. She moves a strand of red hair aside from her face and grins, "Hell, that was an honest accident. Nothing I could do."

Along to Presidio

The three men stare at the feisty woman, and Everett puts his hand to Vic's shoulder to steer him away. Vic looks through the bars at their young brother laid out on the bed. "Doctor, how is he?"

The doctor stands and faces outward to the pair of lawmen and saloon owner waiting outside the holding cell. "We should know better in a day or two."

The doctor wipes his messed hands on a clean towel and puts his basic set of tools beside the leather medical bag. "I put his collarbone back together best I could and patched up his thigh and side." He cleans the blood from the utensils and tries to remove the dark cherry-color stains from his hand. "I'll be back tomorrow to change those bandages in daylight, when I can see better what I'm doing." The oil lamplights flicker as the doctor closes his bag and exits the jail cell.

Everett steps aside, grabs one of the lanterns from the table and raises it up to illuminate Ben's unconscious features. "Anything we can do?"

"Unless you're leaving town, don't move him for now. Make sure he lies still or those wounds will leak."

Vic walks behind the doctor and gives the medical bag a tap as he steps into the front office. "Thanks again, Doc."

The doctor shakes his head with melancholy as he moves to the front door. "I guess I've been seeing you all too often and I'll be back again tomorrow."

Vic opens the door to let the doctor exit and is surprised to see someone standing outside. The doctor tips his hat and slips by into the night, as Vic utters a greeting to the evening caller. "Oh... Hello there, Miss."

The older brother steps aside from the doorway and lets the interior lantern light shine out to reveal the woman waiting, as if about to knock. An odd sense of comfort flickers on Everett's hard features as greets her cordially. "Adeline?"

Vic ushers her inside and the full glow of the lamps illuminates Adeline's features. "Come on in 'n join the party."

Adeline enters the office and looks across the room to where Everett is holding the lantern. Her sparkling eyes quickly drift past him to Tuck, as he turns from the cells in back to face her. The two men at the rear of the office are strangely silent as they return her tentative gaze. Vic guides Adeline through the entryway by the elbow and firmly shuts the door behind her. "Don't mind them. They're still addled if they're gonna shoot each other or not. Can I offer you a seat?"

Vic gestures to an empty chair near the desk and Adeline shakes her head. "No, thank you. I just wanted to see that you are all alright and if there was anything needed."

Tuck finally breaks from his speechless daze and grunts, "Addie... I thought I told you to leave town?"

Everett puts the lantern on the desk and turns to Tuck. "Easy now."

The angered saloon owner ignores the lawman and moves toward Adeline. "It isn't safe here, 'n I told you to go." He stops short of her and hesitantly reaches out his hand. "Come on, I'll take you back to your room. I'll make sure you get on that next stagecoach."

Everett comes up behind Tuck and clears his throat. "You're out of line, Tuckburrow."

The saloon owner turns around and glares at Everett. "I'm out of line?" He glances over at the tin-star on his vest. "You stepped over the line when you and yer kinfolk took on that law-badge to get yer revenge!" A fierce rage shows in Tuck's features as he addresses the brothers in the room. "Since you arrived, this town has been turned into a damned shooting gallery, and you expect it to be safe for womenfolk!?! This is none of your damn business anyhow!"

Along to Presidio

Tuck turns back to Adeline who looks toward Everett. He notices her imploring gaze toward the lawman and growls, "This is no place for any decent kind of folk, and if he cared anything for you, in the least, he would tell you hi'self." He turns his scrutiny on Everett, who remains silent.

In a huff of exasperation, Tuck shakes his head. "Fine!" His annoyance overwhelms him and he throw up his hands. "You're so dammed knowing, then you go 'n protect her." Tuck marches past Adeline and storms outside to the street and the quiet darkness.

Chapter 31

Outside in the night street, Tuck stops to look at the exhibited bodies of Curtis and the other shot-up cowhand. They are both propped up for display on mortician boards fronting the marshal's office. A single oil lamp flickers light on the building front and their blood-encrusted features.

The sound of several horses approaching attracts Tuck's attention, and he slips off to the shadows to observe undetected. The riders gallop up from the black of night, following close at the heels of Dutch Werner. The sullen cattle rancher stops his riders before the jailhouse and the gruesome display of his dead offspring. "Marshal, show yerself!"

The riders spread out across the end of the porch, as Everett appears in the doorway with the sawed-off shotgun. Dutch's horse paws the street, raising a cloud of dust, and the rancher shouts across at the armed lawman on the boardwalk. "What's happened here?" Everett glances aside at the dead bodies of Curtis and the other cowboy put on morbid display. He tucks the short-barreled shotgun under his arm and meets the stare of Dutch and the others. "You're free to take them. There won't be a trial."

Dutch glowers intently at Everett, his mouth agape, barely finding the words as he swells with vengeful passion. "That's my son, goddammit... I want the man who done it!"

Everett brings the stock of the scattergun up to his shoulder and takes a step forward with the barrels leveled. "You'll get nothing of the sort." He aims the gun at the riders. "He was an accomplice in the shooting of an officer of the law and paid for it with his life."

Dutch scowls with a glare at his mounted cowboys, there to back him up. They each sweep their overcoats back to expose holstered sidearms, positioned high on their hips, waiting for the obvious sign to begin the lethal engagement. Everett observes their hostile intent and stands his ground by clicking back both hammers on the double-barreled shotgun. "Gather what you came here for and go." Everett points the barrels of the scattergun at each of the riders and continues, "Or there'll be others to bury."

Dutch stares with spiteful menace at the lone lawman. Without removing his harsh scrutiny from the town marshal, he motions for his cowhands to gather the displayed corpses. "Go on 'n git my boy." Coe and another cowboy grudgingly dismount and step up on the boardwalk. They stand next to Everett as they gather up the lifeless body of Curtis.

Being sure to keep the shotgun aim directed at Dutch, Everett watches them carry the dead body down to the street. They slide the rancher's son over a spare mount and wrestle with the task of fastening the stiff body to the animal's back. Coe looks up at Dutch and then to the other cowboy displayed on the porch. "Ya want us to take Frank along, too?"

The jowly muscles along Dutch's jawline flex and waver in the light. After a moment of consideration, he turns his attentions away from Everett and down to the cowboys. "Tie 'em double." The two cowhands murmur curses under their breath as they try to push one of the rigor mortised legs down to fasten. Dutch snarls as his focus returns to Everett. "The next time we come to town won't be to socialize."

Along to Presidio

Everett remains poised on the boardwalk and lowers the shotgun slightly, as Coe and the other cowboy retrieve the other expired cowhand. He watches them as they struggle to secure the second rigid body alongside like a stack of lumber. From behind the sights of the shotgun, he peers up at Dutch. "It's real bad that things had to go this way. We were only passing through on our way to California."

Unable to restrain his anger any longer, Dutch jabs a pointed finger at Everett and sweeps it across the front porch. "This is far from finished, the way I see it... I'll bury my boy, then I'll be back to murder you and yours." Dutch violently wheels his horse around, jabs his spurred heels and rides off. The mounted cowboys escorting the burdened horse with the double stiffs follow his lead and leave Coe alone in the street, leveling a threatening stare at the lawman. Everett lowers the shotgun slightly but keeps the hammers in the pulled back position until the horseback cowboy finally breaks from the hostile trance and rides away into the black of night.

Everett bends an ear to listen after the group of riders until the sounds of their horse's footfalls fade to the distance. Uncocking the set of hammers, he holds the shotgun in one hand and scans the empty street. Satisfied the threat has past, Everett steps back inside.

As the front door of the marshal's office shuts out the lamp light of the interior, a soft crunch of gravel can be heard from alongside the building. The single lantern and diffused cracks of light that come from around the door and shuttered windows highlight the stained display mounts of the fatalities. From the dim alleyway, the dark figure of Tuck walks away.

Chapter 32

Inside the marshal's office, Everett sets aside the scattergun and barricades the door by fitting a plank across the middle. He glances out the window from the cut-out of the gun-port shutter and sees a shadowy figure cross the empty street. Through the other window, Vic stands guard, holding a rifle. He gives an affirming nod to Everett, who returns the gesture before moving to the rear portion of the office.

Near the entrance to the holding area, Adeline sits in a chair with a cocked pistol cradled across her lap. They both glance to the cell where Ben rests fitfully in one of the bunks. Everett and Adeline stare quietly, as Vic ambles across the room to join them. He touches the bandage around his middle and grunts, "Everything still okay back here?"

Adeline looks at the pair of brothers in the entryway. Her voice is full of concern as she speaks. "He'll come back."

Everett looks at her and replies, "I'll deal with 'em."

Vic slips around his brother and sets the rifle against the horizontal bar on the cell with a clang of metal on metal. "Hey now... We'll all deal with them when they come back." Putting his foot up on a wooden chair seat, he takes a deep, pained breath and inspects the bandage around his ribcage.

Adeline looks over at Ben's freshly bound gun wounds, then up at Vic and the bandage wrapped around his middle. Her apprehensive gaze then travels over to Everett. "How?"

Everett shifts to lean against the doorway, then heaves a sigh. "Come on. I'll walk you back to your room."

The young woman seems irritated that she can't help with the situation. "I'll talk to Hollister for you. He can help."

"Just let it be for now. Let's go."

Everett offers out his hand to Adeline and she stands, still holding the pistol. She looks down at the handgun despondently before she uncocks it and sets it on the chair. "I'll be leaving on the next coach so you won't have to worry any about me." Everett glances over at Vic, who listens and bows his head in agreement.

Standing at the threshold to the jail, Everett looks away. "That's probably a good idea." The ease of the remark seems to pain her, but she remains steady. The lawman quickly assesses both of his wounded siblings and tilts his head toward the front door of the office. "I'll get you to the hotel."

Adeline glances around at the trio of Colbert brothers, who all retain an outward appearance of tranquility despite knowing the deadly consequences of the impending conflict. A tear glistens in her eye and she shakes her head, concerned. "We could all be gone from here before that man and his cowboys come back to town for revenge." The room is quiet as Adeline falters, looking down again at the pistol on the seat. She looks at Everett, then over to Vic and almost appears embarrassed by her expressed plan of flight.

Everett waits beyond the jail area in the office and offers out his elbow to escort Adeline home for the evening. He glances to Vic and tilts his head toward the cell bunk. "Watch over him while I return Miss Sonnett to her room." She looks at Everett a long moment, then to Vic and marches past them both toward the front entrance. Adeline lifts the wooden bar that secures the entry, sets it aside and pulls the heavy door open.

Everett exchanges a knowing look with Vic and strides after her. "Hold it. I'll walk you." Adeline pauses at the partially open door and peers past her shoulder to Everett. "I'll probably be safer on my own."

Taking up the rifle again, Vic snorts his agreement and Everett moves to follow. "It's a short distance. I'll walk you."

~*~

The rays of sunshine lift over the horizon to break the grip of night on the no-name border town. From the shaded porch of the Barrelhouse, Tuck leisurely reclines in a chair, having a smoke while watching the wide, unoccupied street. He looks to the side as Adeline exits the hotel with her packed bags in hand. Her gaze travels to the saloon porch. She looks directly at Tuck, then moves away along the boardwalk and turns the corner from the hotel.

~*~

The inside of the marshal's office is struck by a ray of morning sun, displaying Everett sitting quietly at the desk. His thoughts seem to consume him, as he stares blankly out the partly shuttered front windows. The sound of the rope supports creaking on a cot in the jail breaks him from his musings, and Everett notices Charlotte sitting in the near cell.

Everett stands up and strides over to open her jail door. He glances at Vic beside the sleeping form of their brother. Charlotte peers at the lawmen strangely and waits for either of them to say something. Everett returns her probing stare and steps aside from the jail cell doorway. "You can go."

The female stands and gathers her wrinkled skirting. She looks over at Ben laid out in the next cell and then to Vic, who watches her judiciously. She pulls back her shoulders and marches through the office without looking at them again.

The beams of sunlight stream in through the entryway, as the bitter woman swings the door open wide and steps out.

Vic reclines in his chair, watching Everett take hold of the bars to the open cell door. He lifts the deck of cards off the table and thumbs through them. "What did you do that for?"

Everett shifts his gaze to his older brother and shrugs. "She's just a jealous bawd. There's no stock in what she says to anyone around town."

Everett absentmindedly taps his fingertips on the bars. "We know Dutch and his boys will be coming back around and it's best to not have someone in here that could get hurt."

Vic groans as he flexes his torso in the tight bandages. He flips a card out on the table to begin a game of solitaire. "Yaugh… Hate to get anyone hurt." Everett looks to the front door swung wide and stares out to the empty street.

Both brothers turn, as Ben speaks incoherently while shifting to his other side. Vic kindly reaches over to settle and comfort him. He smoothes his hand along the young man's head and wipes away the sweated hair. "Easy there, brother."

Vic looks up at Everett through the crossed cell bars. "It's gonna start to look like that little skirmish between the Mexes 'n Texans when Dutch and his cowpokes show up."

Everett props himself against the wall and rests his hand on the grip of his pistol. "You mean the Alamo?"

"Yeah... When do you think he'll show?"

"Don't know for sure."

Vic turns his attention back to the lineup of his game and flips the remaining top card to complete the setup row. Ben inhales laboriously and eventually lets out a deep breath. The room is quiet, as Everett looks to the open door and the empty street beyond. "Today most likely… or the next."

Vic nods and plays a card. "Good. I hate waiting."

Chapter 33

From the front porch of the barrelhouse saloon, Tuck watches Charlotte cross the street toward him. She mounts the short set of stairs to the boardwalk and averts her gaze from Tuck. He kicks his chair back to lean on the wall, and his eyes twinkle as his whiskered cheeks pull back to an odd smirk. Charlotte steps to the double entry doors and he remarks, "Tell me something darling, 'cause I'm curious."

Charlotte glances down at him. "Tell you what?"

"Where *did* you hear that sort of talk?"

The troublesome woman tries to keep her composure, but finally lowers her head like a scolded child caught in a lie. He spits over the side of the porch, then gazes to the empty street and marshal's office. "One of them Werner boys, huh?"

She stares at the hem of her dress, then guiltily at Tuck. "It was just something I heard."

Tuck continues to stare away and grunts, unconvinced. "Doesn't matter anyhow. It'll all be over soon, I presume." Charlotte moves toward Tuck, and he raises a flat open palm to block her advance. She waits as he gazes off down the uninhabited street. Submissive from the unwelcome reception, she slowly steps around him and walks inside to the cool comfort of the saloon.

~*~

At the far end of town, Adeline is prepared for the anticipated arrival of the scheduled coach and waits at the livery barn. She sits on a bench in front of the stables and contemplates the quiet of a town about to erupt in violence. The stableman looks over the driving wagon she arrived with and pats his newly acquired purchase with admiration.

Through the soles of her boots, she feels the pounding rumble of the hooves of many horses coming from afar. Adeline and the livery man both turn to notice the dust cloud, rising into the sky on the horizon. She watches and counts seven horseback riders who appear to lift from the distant landscape upon their galloping mounts.

Upon entering town, Dutch Werner slows the group of horseback men to a fast trot and glances over at his foreman. Jenks rides beside the cattle rancher, as they continue past the livery shed and stables. The rancher's stern gaze wanders from his riders to Adeline, seated near the shade of the barn. An ominous look of vengeful bereavement clouds his features as the horseback cowboys march past.

Adeline anticipates the impending promise of death while watching the armed group of horsemen ride into battle. One of the saddle animals nickers to another as the cadence of footfalls marches the horseback group onto the street of town. Their looming path of destruction is followed by a cloud of clinging dust coming up from the dry thoroughfare.

~*~

The town is quiet and still as Dutch leads his cowboys down the street and veers toward the saloon. Seated in the porch shade, Tuck watches the group stop at the hitching post rail and witnesses two of the cowboys dismount to go inside. He pins his ear back to listen to their conversation after they order several bottles of liquid courage.

From the shadows, the saloon owner sits and stares across at the rancher in the center of the lineup of cowhands. The old, creaky chair rocks forward and Tuck coughs smugly, "Only two of yer boys thirsty today?"

Dutch's eyes squint into the shade from the bright sunlight as he hisses, "You a part of this, Tuckburrow?"

Tuck smirks at the cattle boss and rubs his hand across his cheek innocently. "Don't know... Am I?"

Dutch studies the saloon owner seated in the shadows, while the sweated mounts mingle against each other at the hitch rail. "You'll have no more porch sittin' time if you are." Tuck continues to comb his bearded chin and watches the cowboys exit the saloon with a pair of whiskey bottles each. They both toss the extra bottles to a rider in the lineup and grab for the reins of their mounts.

Tuck watches from the porch as they swing into their saddles and wait for orders from the hard-nosed rancher. Dutch tilts his head away and eases his horse into the street. Practically in unison, the gang of mounted cowboys steers away from the saloon and faces toward the mission church.

Positioned at the center of the town, Dutch glances from the Barrelhouse to the marshal's office across the street. Tuck calls out to him mockingly, "Y'all having a picnic?"

Waving the mounted riders onward, Dutch sidesteps his mount toward the saloon and glares at Tuck on the porch. "Yer not invited...Understood?" The two exchange a hard stare until Dutch finally spurs his horse and lopes off toward the cowboys gathering near the mission church.

As the dust in the street settles, Tuck sees the riders assemble at the churchyard, and he turns his attentions across the street to the marshal's office. Standing in the open door, Everett watches the group of cowboys and looks to the saloon. Their gazes linger, until Everett steps back inside the building.

~*~

A warm afternoon breeze blows through the trees, while Dutch Werner and his cowboys congregate in the sparse shade around the dilapidated church. They pass the whiskey bottles around and take several pulls from the shared jugs. Jenks stands beside Dutch and watches the men attempt to bolster their nerves. "We shouldn't let 'em get too far on their drink, or they won't be able to stand up, let alone shoot."

"We'll get 'em just drunk enough to where they have some fire in their belly and won't run."

Jenks looks from Dutch to each of the familiar faces. "How far do you actually want to take this whole thing?"

Dutch turns to Jenks with a look of wonderment, then stares down the street and growls, "I'm gonna put all them brothers dead in the ground. If I'm not feelin' satisfied after that, I'll go 'n shoot ol' Tuckburrow there for good measure."

Jenks casts a look away from the crazed ranch owner. "We might be burying a few of our own, as well."

Dutch walks over and brusquely grabs the remainder of a whiskey bottle away from one of the drinking cowboys. He returns to the foreman and thrusts the glass vessel at Jenks. "You best be puttin' up some of this, too. Make no mistake… The death of my boy will be avenged to the very last man."

Jenks takes the jug by the neck and puts it to his mouth. The ranch foreman takes a long swallow of the contents and hands it back over to his boss. Dutch stares hard at Jenks a long moment and then looks off again down the vacant street. His faraway gaze possesses a fanatical, bereavement that no man would want to cross.

Chapter 34

The inside of the marshal's office is cool and shady behind the partially closed door and gun-port shuttered windows. Everett moves from the cut-out portion of a secured window to the wall hung gun rack and takes down a Winchester rifle. Putting the long gun across his lap, he sits behind the desk and opens a container of cartridges on the wooden surface. The shiny brass casings tumble and roll from the pile on the desk and point in all directions.

The only sound in the room is the click of the loading gate on the receiver after Everett thumbs a blunt nosed cartridge into the rifle. He looks across the forted-up office toward his brother seated on a chair against the back wall. "There's seven of them."

Vic looks to the partial deck of cards nearby and snorts. "What about Tuck?"

Everett dumps a few more rounds from the box of cartridges on the desk and thumbs them steadily into the rifle. "That ass-head just sold 'em bottles of liquid pluck."

Vic can't help but let a smirk appear on his features. He fingers the tatty deck of cards on the table next to him and murmurs, "He said our business wouldn't interfere with his." Everett returns his sibling's grin at the shared understanding and thumbs the last loaded cartridge into the rifle to top it off.

A shadow sweeps past the light in the window, and there is a quiet knock at the door before it swings slowly open.

The loaded Winchester is quickly levered with a round and Everett has it aimed along the desktop, pointed outside. The office door opens wide to reveal a group of men gathered in front of the jailhouse. Everett winces into the sunlight as the figures crowd around the door but remain on the walkway. "Are you here for a committee meeting?"

Lonie, the barber, slowly steps into the marshal's office to see Everett with a rifle at the desk and Vic seated opposite. The eldest brother takes his pistol from the holster rig sitting on the card table nearby, thumbs opens the side gate on the revolver to check the load and snaps it back again. "Something on your mind, fella?"

The mild-mannered barber stands in the bright sunlit doorway and fidgets nervously, as he looks over his long-haired shoulder to the assembled group on the boardwalk. From his vantage behind the desk, Everett can see some of the townsfolk carrying single-shot rifles, loose-powder pistols and muzzle-loading shotguns. Lonie starts to speak, stops to clear his throat and begins again. "We saw the bunch of hired ranch hands that Dutch brought with him to town. We've assembled a town vigilance committee to back you." Everett leans forward on the desktop without getting up from the chair to peer out at the ill-equipped vigilantes.

None of the citizens look too eager or ready for action. He lowers the aim of the repeater rifle and lets his gaze fall on the pre-Civil War era percussion rifle held at Lonie's side. "That's fine, but we don't plan to have much trouble with them yet. There's no need to get anyone else hurt."

The long-haired barber looks out the doorway to the churchyard and back. He fidgets with the antique rifle at his side and questions anxiously. "Uh, are you sure about that?"

Along to Presidio

Everett nods and pushes back in the chair with a creak. "I'd rather not have a throng of untrained gunman on my hands to deal with." Lonie nods his approval sheepishly. Everett uncocks the rifle, lays it across the desk and queries the reluctant barber. "Is Tuckburrow out there with you?"

Lonie pushes a strand of hair behind his ear and tilts his head to the saloon. "He's sitting o'er at the Barrelhouse."

Vic places his pistol aside on the table and snorts. "That's mighty helpful of 'im."

The barber looks over at Vic and shrugs somewhat. "He said that someone has to take care of business in town."

Leaning forward, Everett fingers one of the loose cartridges spilled out on the desk. "Well, get these folks back to their own business, and we'll take care of Dutch and his."

With an audible sigh of relief, Lonie exits the doorway and Everett stands by the desk to watch the crowd disperse. He reaches over to the gun rack and takes down another rifle. Lifting a booted foot up to place on the seat of the chair, Everett looks across the room to the jail in back and then to Vic. "You have anything to say 'bout any of this?"

"It's your call little brother."

Everett scoops up a handful of cartridge rounds and thumbs them into the empty rifle's receiver, one after another.

~*~

The small group of townsmen fronting the marshal's office quickly disbands and scatters from sight. Bemused, Tuck watches from the Barrelhouse porch and snorts, "Chicken-shit bastards..." He stands, kicks his chair away on the porch stoop and walks down the steps to the street. Looking toward the mission church at the far end of town, he can make out the small gathering of Dutch Werner's cowboys. With a groan, he slowly makes the short walk across the street to the marshal's office.

~*~

The front door of the office swings inward with a kick and Everett and Vic look up to see Tuck's outline in the entry. They relax the ready grip on their weapons, holding their fire while the figure stands and peers around the dimly lit room. Everett stands beside the desk and keeps the freshly-loaded rifle at his waistline. "Need something, Tuck?"

Tuck glances down the street toward the churchyard, steps into the office and leans on the iron handle of the door. "Just thinking how this place mostly went unused when Polk was the law hereabouts. It was downright peaceable then."

Everett sets the rifle down and commences to load a handgun while Vic leaves his pistol in easy reach and lays out a card game. He flips an ace of clubs on the incomplete deck and grunts, "Probably a lot of things are different."

Tuck takes another step inside the office to look around the opened door at Vic positioned near the back wall. "And still a' changin'."

Everett finishes loading the handgun, as he moves around to the front of the desk and props a hip to the edge. "What do you want here, Tuck?"

The saloon owner frowns as he looks away from Vic with the cards. "You want my help?"

Everett lays the pistol on the desk. "Is this your fight?"

Tuck walks over and picks up the gun from the desk. He looks it over in his hand, brings the hammer to half-cock and rolls the cylinder. "Damn you for sending away that vigilance committee." Tuck twirls the revolver and smiles. "I'm the one that got it together for you."

Everett walks to the threshold of the rear cell area and picks up the short-barreled shotgun positioned in the corner. He snaps open the breach, inspects the double load of shot shells and returns the gun to the leaned position on the wall.

He turns to address Tuck. "A mob of armed men are good for intimidation, but when it comes to action, they're a mess."

Tuck eyes the pair of lawmen occupying the room. "Maybe a bit of intimidation is all them cowpokes need."

Everett glances aside at Vic thumbing the deck of cards. "Might work on the hired hands, but Dutch is out for blood to avenge the death of his kin."

Tuck winks, "Same as you?" Everett remains silent in response to the candid remark, and Tuck cocks and uncocks the revolver in his hand. "Well, Lonie was relieved anyway."

The two brothers exchange a ready glance and Vic pitches the handful of cards in a pile on the table and stands. Fidgeting a bit in his chest bandage, Vic pulls on his vest and buttons it up the front. He speaks out with his chin lowered. "When the shooting starts, it's best to have professionals at our backs, or we're as likely to get shot as the other guy." Finishing the row of vest buttons, Vic pulls on his coat and Everett tosses him one of the loaded rifles.

Tuck grimaces through his whiskers as he slips the loaded revolver in his coat pocket and moves back to the front door of the marshal's office. "Let's go 'n get to talking." Everett assesses the somewhat improved odds, as Tuck steps to the boardwalk and into the sunlight. He puts on his broad-brimmed hat and grabs the other loaded rifle from the desk. Following Tuck outside, the gunmen stand silhouetted in the door opening, prepared to address their fate.

Chapter 35

As the heat of day hangs heavy, the saloon owner and two brothers walk the boardwalk in front of the marshal's office. In unison, they descend the short set of stairs and the dry dusty street swirls around the shafts of their tall boots. Positioned shoulder to shoulder, the three gunmen make the lethal march toward the imminent conflict.

In the churchyard of the mission, one of the cowboys stands near the tied horses in the street and gazes into town. He looks to the others milling in the shade and gives a whistle. "Here they come…" Dutch and the others turn their attention in the direction of the saloon and jailhouse to observe the three men walking toward them.

Dutch ponders their approach and inferior numbers. When one of the cowboys starts to take a drink, the ranch boss reaches out and snatches the whiskey bottle from his hand. "Better hitch yer pistol belts up, 'cause there's a fight comin'." Dutch aggressively tosses the bottle away to break against the tumble-down picket fencing surrounding the churchyard.

The five cowboys come over to gather behind Dutch and Jenks, as the three men advance from the marshal's office. The old cattle rancher looks past his shoulder and calls out to one of his cowboys. "Coe… Git in position with yer rifle." Dutch angles his head toward the church tower, and the cowboy slips back from the group to the mission building.

The foreman watches the hired hand gain entrance through the side doorway of the church and nods to Dutch. "He's inside. We still got the numbers on 'em and probably won't need him up there."

Dutch glowers ahead, intently focused on the trio of men walking nearer to confront them. "Jenks... I don't give a damn 'bout fair, just so they're all dead when we're done."

~*~

Across town at the livery barn and stagecoach depot, Adeline paces back and forth in the street. She tries to get a distant glimpse of the confrontation from one angle, then marches across the road to attempt a view from the other side. The looming suspense of the fight begins to weigh on her imagination, as she looks to her luggage piled just under the shade of the depot porch.

~*~

Pacing toward the churchyard, Tuck and Vic stride at Everett's side as they near the group of armed cowboys. Dutch and his hired hands fan out in front of the mission. Tuck clutches the spare pistol concealed in his coat pocket, takes a quick headcount of their opposition and speaks aside. "There was seven of them that come into town this mornin'."

Tuck stares ahead to Dutch and Jenks at center, as Everett and Vic count the cowboys to the side. Everett sweeps back his coat tail to uncover his sidearm and puts both hands ready on the Winchester rifle. "I count six. Watch your backs."

The three approach the church and Dutch greets them. "Tuckburrow... You low-down, under-handed son-of-a-bitch. I thought we agreed this wasn't your deal?"

Tuck shrugs innocently and halfway grins at Dutch. "Figured I'd jump in and play this game out."

The rancher clenches his jaw hard and turns to Everett. "How 'bout you Marshal? You ready to play this hand out?"

Everett stands firm with his coat pulled back and the rifle held across his chest. "You and your boys need to leave this town to the good folks who want to live here peaceable."

Dutch seems surprised, almost amused, as he gestures to the collected men beside him. "*We* need to leave?"

Everett nods and lets his eyes scan the lineup of whiskey-bolstered ranch hands. He speaks with a low and firm tone. "This could be a decent town someday. I cain't have you and them causing any more of a disturbance here."

"A decent town? Damn horse-shit... I *made* this town!" Dutch sets his hand along the butt of his holstered revolver, leans forward toward Everett and growls, "Who are you to tell me to leave? This place was nothing before I put it here."

Everett remains unmoved in his stance and responds, "Now it'll do better without you."

Dutch lets the comment burn down inside and growls, "We come here to get the man who murdered my boy."

Everett remains stoic as he stares toward the rancher. "He was killed in self-defense by an officer of the law."

Dutch can hardly contain his temper as he thunders, "To hell with you and yer brothers! You think you can come to my town and try to say what's lawful?"

Vic stands beside Everett and has his rifle half-raised. "Go on home Dutch, while you still can."

The rancher glances at Vic, assesses his condition and then turns back to Everett. "There has got to be some kind of justice served for my boy. We'll give the killer a fair trial."

Everett shakes his head, but his stare remains focused. "There will be no trial by you or yourn."

Dutch glares at Everett as he moves ominously closer. "Then we'll take him." The rancher calls aside, "Payson... Jubal... Go 'n get him." Two of the hired hands separate from the group and swing wide of the lawmen, heading for the jail.

Everett watches them move around to the side and stares hard at Dutch. "Tell them to stop."

Jenks moves nearer to the opposing faction and scoffs, "The one laid up in the jail was shot up pretty good, I hear." He winks, "We'd just be putting him out of his misery."

Everett looks to his periphery as the two hired hands make a wide arc past them, and he tilts his head to his brother. "Vic... Go 'n stop 'em."

The older brother holds the rifle at his hip and begins to slowly back away, still watching the men they are faced off to. The tension mounts, and Everett lets his rifle drop down in his left hand as his right moves toward the pistol hung at his side. "Call them off, Dutch." There is complete silence except the soft crunch of the gravel from the street underfoot, as Vic and the two cowboys move toward the marshal's office.

Everett's eyes slowly drift to each of the armed men fanned out before him as he settles on Dutch. "Stop 'em now, or I'll burn you down right here."

The old rancher looks past Everett to the cowboys already on the porch of the jailhouse. A cruel smile spreads across his lips as he faces the sole lawman and saloon owner. "Go ahead! Bring 'im out boys!"

Everett clenches his jaw as he glances over his shoulder to Vic and the cowboys at the door then back again to Dutch. Tuck keeps his hand buried in his coat pocket and seems calm, collected and patient. He stares straight ahead at Jenks and speaks to Everett in a low whisper. "Let me get Jenks."

Everett keeps his attention on Dutch as, over his shoulder, the rancher observes the cowboys on the boardwalk. Everett puts his finger through the trigger guard on his holstered sidearm and wraps his hand around the pistol grip. "I mean it Dutch. There won't be another warning from me."

The thumb on Everett's hand eases down over the hammer. "It doesn't have to come to this."

Dutch returns his look to Everett and Tuck, then sneers, "You're both done here. This is my town."

Behind, moving stiff with pain, Vic is almost to the marshal's office as the cowboys prepare to enter the doorway. Everett stares at Dutch with a sense of heightened awareness. Tuck glances behind to the men at the jailhouse and shrugs amiably toward Jenks. "Let's see what you got, Jenks."

"Anytime, Hollie …"

Tuck makes a feigned move with his right hand to his holstered sidearm and simultaneously pulls the concealed pistol from his left coat pocket. With the hideaway revolver cocked, he takes deliberate aim at Jenks and pulls the trigger. The pistol shot goes directly into the ranch foreman's middle chest as he attempts to pull his gun which fires prematurely. The wild shot from Jenks' firearm whizzes past Tuck's boot, before he has a chance to fire another shot from the hideaway. A look of deceived shock twists on the ranch foreman's features as he stumbles back with the deadly chest wound and cocks his pistol a second time.

Chapter 36

In front of the marshal's office, Vic hears the opening shots of the fight and quickly fires off the rifle at one of the cowboys. The first to the door, Payson, takes a bullet hit to his mid-chest and spins away against the front windows of the building. Still moving forward at a steady pace, Vic levers his rifle and lets off another shot at the other cowboy. Jubal ducks under the blast on the adobe wall near the doorway and dives inside.

~*~

The pistol hangs limp in the hand of the ranch foreman, discharging into the street, and Jenks stares ahead with a blank expression as he drops the smoking gun and crumples. A rifle shot whizzes past, through Everett's coat tail, and he looks up to see Coe in the bell tower of the mission church. Everett jerks his revolver from the holster and looks to Dutch as the rancher shoots a missing shot at the opposing twosome. Raising his pistol, Everett returns fire and hits Dutch along his outstretched forearm.

Tuck looks upward and directs his aim to the tower as Coe sends a torrent of rifle shots down upon the street. Several rounds of bullet lead whiz past the two rivals and kick up pinging clouds of dust in the street. Despite the disadvantaged odds, Everett and Tuck stand their ground, choosing their next mark.

Faced-off against the group of cowboy adversaries, Everett retains his stance and methodically fires his revolver. One of the targeted cowhands drops to the ground dead, while another grabs at his wounded abdomen still attempting to engage his pistol in the street fight. Multiple gunshots are exchanged, until Everett clicks his gun on an empty chamber. He holsters his expended handgun and notices Dutch slip behind a short adobe wall to shoot from cover.

Rifle shots continue to rain down from the bell tower and Tuck discharges the last remaining shots in his handgun. He pockets the spent hideaway gun, draws his sidearm from his hip holster and hollers over at Everett alongside him. "He's a damn poor shot up there, but he's bound to get lucky... Get out of the street!" Everett puts his rifle to use, shooting and moving to the cover of an unhitched wagon. Splinters of wood shatter away from a bullet-hit at the side of the wagon, as Everett levers another rifle shot toward Dutch, positioned behind the mud-brick wall.

~*~

The spent black powder-smoke wafts down the street and there is a momentary lull in the gunfight. Everett takes the opportunity to reload his handgun from the loose handful of cartridges in his coat pocket as he looks around for Vic. Across the street from the jail, positioned behind a rain barrel, Vic fires his rifle. A shot from the tower splinters a chunk off the wagon near Everett's head, and he calls across the street. "Careful Vic! They got one at the top of the church!"

The older brother levers several rifle shots into the front jamb of the marshal's office as Jubal ducks away, out of sight. Vic briefly pops his head up from behind the shot-up rain barrel and gives Everett a wave. He quickly drops down to cover again, as several more gunshots are fired his way.

Along to Presidio

Finished reloading his firearm, Everett assesses their present situation. He looks over at Tuck, who keeps down in a laid out position behind the churchyard fence. Several rifle shots hail from above, forcing the saloon owner to stay low with his belly to the ground. Annoyed, Tuck peeks over at Everett, shaking his head. "That's Coe in the bell tower…"

Squatted on the far side of the low adobe wall, Dutch peeks over, shoots his pistol and hollers to Tuck and Everett. "He's got enough ammunition to stay up there all damn day. Give 'im up to us, and we might let you live."

Everett pokes the barrel of his rifle over the wagon and sends two more shots toward Dutch, causing him to duck down. The mud wall shatters away over Dutch's head, as he scrambles away for better shelter at the mission church. Everett sights a bead at the mid-center of the fleeing man's turned back, but grudgingly holds the intended rifle shot. "Dutch! Call off your men and we'll end all this."

~*~

Concealed behind a buttress of the adobe constructed church, Dutch cradles his forearm and reloads his revolver. He peers around the corner to get a clearer view of Jubal shooting from the open doorway of the marshal's office. Without exposing himself to the deadly aim of his opponents, the ranch boss calls out to his hired man in the jailhouse. "Jubal? You hear me boy?"

The exchange of shots in the street ceases momentarily. A gentle breeze blows the dissipated puffs of spent powder-smoke in a drifting haze down the wide avenue of town. Dutch calls out again, a bit louder, "Jubal?"

"Yeah, Dutch?"

"Is he in there?"

There is a long pause before Jubal responds, "Who?"

Agitated, Dutch glances down at his lowered gun and bloodied forearm as he shakes his head. He eases around the corner of the mission building as far as he can without being a target and hollers out again to his man, this time much louder. "That other brother who kilt Curtis, that's *who!*"

There is a hiatus of gunfire as everyone reloads their emptied firearms and waits for the fighting to commence. Jubal pokes his rifle barrel out from the doorway and calls over toward the mission church. "Yeah, he's here in back…"

Dutch ejects a spent brass shell casing and slips in another round from his vest pocket. He looks to where Everett hides behind the wagon and Tuck lays low by the fence row. "Shoot him then. Ya hear me boy? Shoot him!"

Everett turns to face the marshal's office and judges the wide open, defenseless expanse. Another barrage of rifle shots comes down on the wagon from the bell tower, and splinters of broken wood scatter around. His gaze connects with his brother across the street by the broken barrel, and he calls out, "Stop him, Vic!"

From down at ground level, behind the church fence, Tuck watches as Vic hastily rushes across the street toward the front entry of the marshal's office. Two consecutive rifle shots ring out from the bell tower and Vic winces then stumbles before dropping to one knee. Everett moves away from the old wagon and dashes into the street to provide cover for Vic. The older brother clutches the gunshot to his lower leg and tries to stand upright as he witnesses Everett rushing nearer. "I'm fine… Go 'n protect Ben!"

Everett alters his route of travel as persistent rifle shots from the church tower skitter off the open street around him. Dragging himself onward with the injured leg, Vic watches Everett take a leap to the boardwalk, fronting the jailhouse.

Along to Presidio

There is a muffled blast of a discharged shotgun that echoes from inside the jailhouse, promptly followed by another.

Everett stutter-steps to a standstill as the envisioned consequence of the two blasts take hold of his imagination. "No, Ben... No!" A suspenseful instant passes until Jubal stumbles backwards out from the marshal's office doorway. The cowboy spins to reveal his blood-spattered chest and face. Lowering his handgun, Jubal drops to the boardwalk, dead.

Chapter 37

Inside the jail cell at the rear of the marshal's office, Adeline stands beside Ben, holding the shotgun raised to her shoulder. She cracks the breech and ejects the two blackened shot-shells, as the smoke lingers upward from the recent discharge. Reaching to the nearby table, she grabs two fresh rounds, plunks them in the side by side chambers and snaps it closed.

The two brothers converge outside the jailhouse over the dead bodies of the shot-up cowboys lying on the porch. Vic hobbles painfully toward the entryway to lean on it for support and suddenly another bullet tears into him from afar. He grunts and winces while grasping for a grip on the doorframe with his blood-covered hand.

Disregarding the plinking of rifle lead showering down around them, Everett rushes to Vic's side. "Hold on, brother. Gotta git you inside." They step around the dead cowboy and over the slumped body of Jubal spread across the threshold. Tossing themselves inside, they move out of sight-range from the hostile gunfire coming down from the bell tower.

Tuck sits upright by the fence-row and takes careful aim with his revolver at the high perch on the mission tower. Well-positioned above the street, Coe pokes his head up, levers his rifle and aims it at the jailhouse porch. In an instant, the hot burn of bullet lead rips across Tuck's raised hand just as he squeezes off the shot that tags Coe in the bell tower.

He turns to the side of the churchyard to see Dutch grinning with vengeful delight as he clicks back the hammer on his pistol to shoot off another round in Tuck's direction. Tuck squeezes off a pistol shot, aimed at Dutch and ducks back down behind the stick fence. He inspects his bloodied hand and grumbles, "Dutch, you damned bastard."

~*~

Everett pulls Vic further inside the marshal's office and eases him on the floor, just past the bright swath of sunlight coming from the open doorway. "Now, you hold still Vic."

The older brother groans with his newly inflicted wounds and motions to the back cells. "What about Ben?"

Everett looks to the lockup and calls out, "Ben…?"

Surprisingly, a female responds from the rear jail cell. "I'm here, Everett." Adeline appears in the pass-through doorway and Everett gawks at her with a stunned gratitude. From the tower, high above, a rifle bullet smashes through the front window shutter and another gunshot promptly follows, skittering across the plank floor just inside the doorway.

The side loading gate on Everett's revolver snaps open and he lets the empty brass shell casings tumble to the wood-plank floor at his feet. He moves to the desk, dumps out another box of cartridges and shoves a handful in his pocket. Sliding several fresh rounds into the cylinder of his six-gun, he looks behind at Adeline standing by his wounded brother. "I need you to stay here with Vic and Ben."

Everett steps to the doorway and peeks outside to the smoke-hazed street. He studies the shooter's position in the mission church tower and his gaze travels down to the form of Tuck concealed behind a flimsy, broken picket-fence row. Looking behind at Adeline, the two exchange a mutual look of compassion for the pinned-down saloon owner.

~*~

Along to Presidio

The stagnant air in the street is thick with the rotten-egg smell of burnt, black-powder smoke lingering like a fog. Two cowboys at the back of the mission church mount their horses and gallop away behind the abandoned structure. Several other of the untethered saddle-mounts drift free of the picket line, heading away from the source of gunfire.

During a temporary lull, Everett scans the town and the bell tower high above. He walks outside to the porch and steps down to the street, aware of being a prime target. Quickly, Everett makes his way toward the churchyard fence and Tuck's laid out position there. The lever action of a cocking rifle can be distinctly heard from behind as someone steps from the boardwalk in front of the marshal's office.

Everett intuitively glances up to the bell tower first, then back at the woman with the rifle behind him in the street. "Dammit Adeline! You need to stay inside!" He waves her back, but she has a look of hard determination as she gazes past Everett to see Tuck leaned up against the church-yard fence with a bloody arm across his chest. She stares at the two men across from her and shoots the rifle up at the tower. Cocking the rifle again, she yells down the street at them both, "I will not stand by while you both try to get yourself killed."

Their attention is drawn to the pounding sound of galloping horses coming around the corner from the church. Now mounted, Dutch and his last remaining cowboy spur horseback down the main street toward Everett and Adeline. Each mounted rider has a pistol in hand, as they bear down on the two standing in their path.

Everett stands his ground attempting to block Adeline. She keeps her rifle raised and shoots over Everett's head, tagging the charging cowboy riding behind Dutch in the lead. She cocks the rifle again, but the lever loop jams open wide with a cartridge stuck in the receiver.

The running horses continue toward Everett at a thundering gallop, and the lawman points his pistol at the wounded cowboy, then redirects it over to Dutch Werner. Tuck sits back against the fence-row, raises is handgun and fires off his last three remaining rounds, which tumbles the already wounded cowboy from the saddle. The dead rider hits the street and the empty saddle horse charges past while Everett fires his pistol at Dutch, thumbing back the hammer to shoot again as the rancher gallops closer. Simultaneously, Dutch returns a shot at Everett, but the bullet whizzes past the lawman, grazing his coat sleeve.

Still horseback, Dutch follows the emptied mount past Everett and reins up as he nears the woman standing with the jammed rifle. Everett spins on his boot heel and draws a bead on Dutch, as the rancher slows his horse just before Adeline. Everett holds back the hammer on the revolver and watches, as Dutch slumps forward against the saddle horn.

The rancher's horse eases to an ambling walk and slowly turns to face back toward the lawman in the street. Adeline steps forward to follow until Everett calls out to her, "Adeline, stay where you're at." She stops and witnesses the wilting figure of Dutch Werner as he wanders toward Everett. The lawman maintains his position and keeps his gun arm raised as he waits for his defeated adversary to step nearer.

The body-laden saddle-mount stops in the middle of the street, and Dutch slowly lifts his head to confront Everett. The deep creases on the old cattleman's features show the tough times of hard-fought years on the West Texas frontier. His face suddenly drops the hard edge as he stares at Everett. "You've kilt me…"

Everett lowers his arm with the pistol aim and returns the lingering stare of the dying, horseback figure before him. "You brought this upon yerself."

Dutch coughs, then sputters a few softly spoken words. "...bury me with my boys."

Everett nods, and Dutch gapes blankly a long moment until his head falls limp. From behind the idle saddle mount, Adeline steps away with the jammed rifle still in her hands. She looks to Dutch collapsed over the fork of his saddle and tosses the fouled, open-lever rifle away from her to the street. Her attention instantly returns to the churchyard fence where Tuck droops awkwardly.

Everett turns to look at Tuck and notices he has several serious-looking wounds. He raises a hand up to Adeline and gestures for her to stay put. "Stay here just a moment." Adeline resists his proposal and takes a step toward Tuck, before Everett places his hand on her arm. "Please wait..."

She breaks her stare on the wounded man and looks into Everett's eyes. The two connect with a communal understanding and Adeline takes a deep, calming breath. Slowly, she nods her reluctant consent and watches as Everett approaches Tuck at the fence-row of the mission churchyard.

Chapter 38

With measured steps, still aware of the hostile surroundings, Everett walks to the spot where Tuck is slumped along the churchyard fence. "Tuck?" A rasping breath his heard from the saloon owner as he heaves his wounded torso in reply, "Yeah, Marshal...?" Everett walks over and stands before the wounded figure leaned against the line of pickets.

Tuck clutches his blood-splattered hands across his upper abdomen wound and winces in pained discomfort. Everett stares down at the dying saloon owner, recognizing the mortal seriousness of the inflicted gut-shot, bullet wound. "I'll get you a doctor."

Tuck turns his head to the side and gives a gurgled chest cough. "My lungs is filling up."

Everett turns back to the apprehensive young woman standing in the street next to Dutch, who is dead in the saddle. Tuck acknowledges Everett's obvious thought about Adeline and shake his unshaven chin. "If you have any compassion for me, don't you let her come over and see me this way."

Adeline starts to advance on them, and Everett raises his open palm, motioning for her to halt. He returns his attentions back to Tuck and crouches to a position at eye level. "What can I do for you, Tuck?"

"The cards are on the table…" Tuck clears his throat. "My hand is nearly all played out." The saloon owner gives another blood-filled cough and takes a laborious breath.

Everett still holds his revolver and looks down at the lethal instrument of destruction. He mournfully looks at Tuck and tries to offer some sort of consoling words. "You got 'im."

Tuck winces with a swell of increasing pain and grins. "Was aiming for Dutch… That other one jest got in the way."

The fatally wounded saloon owner motions for the lawman to come nearer, and Everett squats down even lower. "Do something for me, will ya?" Tuck whispers gruffly, as he forces his last words out through wound-compromised lungs. "Git her to go back East to where she come from, if you can." Everett leans in closer as Tuck coughs his throat clear to speak. "She is a strong-willed girl."

"She is a strong-willed woman."

Tuck tries to quell a fit of coughing and musters up the strength to continue, "This is no place for a daughter of mine." Everett nods silently and watches the man before him slowly lose the spirit of life. He stares at Tuck until the dying man's final words begin to settle in. "Your daughter…?"

Tuck smiles with a weakening cough and his eyes suddenly sparkle with pride. "She has her mother's looks."

"And your grit."

Tuck has another raspy fit of coughing and reaches out to hold onto Everett's arm. "She does seem to be stubborn." The waning saloon owner chokes for air and holds tight to the man kneeled before him. "Are you my friend?"

Everett dips his chin as his eyes glisten with an affectionate emotion. "Yeah, Tuck… I'm your friend."

Tuck gives a heaving cough that brings fresh clots of blood up from his lungs. He spits the red lifeblood aside, wipes his mouth and tries to catch his failing breath of air. Everett looks to Tuck's blood-covered hands and pats them. The dying man gazes up at Everett, nods and sighs serenely. "Knew it from the first."

Kneeled down at Tuck's side, Everett watches the man finally slip away. A long moment passes before he stands and looks around at the morose town surroundings... from the church bell tower, to the slain bodies fronting the marshal's office, to Dutch still slumped horseback and finally to Adeline standing alone in the street, watching him.

The sudden quiet of the town is unnerving following the ear-splitting commotion from the gun battle in the street. Everett looks momentarily down at his firearm, sweeps his coat back from his side and tucks it in the holster at his hip. He stands and faces the woman opposite him, and they seem at a loss for any sort of meaningful exchange.

Chapter 39

A time has passed, and the streets of the nameless border town have been swept clear of the gory remnants of violence. On the shaded porch of the Barrelhouse, Adeline sits in Tuck's habitual chair, supervising firsthand new any activity in town. She casually observes as Everett approaches on horseback, followed by both his brothers in the familiar, four-wheeled carriage that had brought her to town, weeks prior.

Everett rides up and stops in front of the Barrelhouse. He sits tall in the saddle and peers into the shaded overhang toward the young woman seated on the porch. In the street, the two brothers sit beside each other fronting the buggy's former owner. She leans forward in the chair, rises and steps out to the edge of the boardwalk. "So, you all are leaving?"

Everett looks across at her and nods without a sound. They exchange a fond look of admiration, until he looks up at the sign above the saloon porch that reads *Tuck's Barrelhouse*. He shifts in the saddle and frowns. "You going to keep it?"

Adeline's eyes shimmer in return as she smiles wide. "Yes, I guess, I'll just have to get used to the moniker of *Tuck*." The young woman looks to Vic and Ben seated on the bench of the carriage and bends to pick up a basket of provisions. Adeline gracefully steps down from the shaded porch, smiles up at the set of brothers and hands them the package of food.

The newly ordained saloon proprietor takes a lasting look at Vic and Ben in their most recent bandaging and nods. "You will each need to take care of the other in California."

Vic flexes his chest near his almost healed wound. "Hear tell, most folks are nicer there and don't shoot at you."

Ben flashes his boyish grin and tips his hat to Adeline. "Much obliged, you lookin' out for me during that fracas." She steps back from the forward wheel of the wagon and returns his smile in kind.

The eldest brother nods appreciatively and shifts the leather lead-lines of the harnessed horse through his fingers. "You take care of yerself now, Miss." Vic gives a firm toss of the reins and looks down the street. "Hayah! Git up there." Ben glances from Adeline to Everett, who still sits horseback, as the wheeled carriage slowly rolls forward through town. "You still plan on coming with us, Everett?"

The remaining brother waves them both off as they travel away down the open street westward. "I'll catch up." He watches them and then returns his attentions to Adeline. She gazes up at him silently while he turns his horse to leave, stares forward and hesitates. Unsure, he looks down at her, then swings his leg over to dismount. Standing in the street, face to face, Everett stumbles over choosing his precise words. "I... I don't know what to say."

Everett removes his hat, holds it before him and fidgets with the wide brim. After a long, uncomfortable pause, Adeline takes control of the awkward encounter and speaks, "I have no plans of moving back East, if that's what you were going to plead again. I hope to make a life for myself here."

Everett chews his lip and looks down the town's street. "I can think of better places."

Adeline follows Everett's passing gaze to the marshal's office, then to the old mission and shrugs. "Here's a start."

Along to Presidio

The creaking turn of wagon wheels and the clomping sound of hooves fade, as the horse and buggy roll out of town. Everett turns his gaze to the surrounding buildings, as his brothers travel their path west. "I guess I have to go with 'em. Had my mind set on it once, and I've got to see it through."

Adeline peers past Everett's shoulder to the departing travelers and then puts on a nice smile for the former lawman. "If you make it back this way, might still be a job for you." The heartfelt smile slowly fades from her features as she adds, "I will most likely still be around."

Everett lowers his chin and extends his hand to her. "It's been a pleasure, Miss Sonnett."

Adeline reaches out her slight hand and casually takes hold of his to shake. "Take care, Everett." There is a peaceful quiet all around as they retain their grip in front of the saloon.

Everett releases her hand and murmurs. "Adeline."

The ex-lawman puts on his hat and goes to his horse. He glances back at her with a lasting fondness as he raises his foot to the stirrup, steps to the saddle and swings a leg over. Looking to the horizon, Everett spots a man working at constructing something near the road, at the edge of town.

Everett glances down at Adeline, still standing in the street before the Barrelhouse saloon and finally looks away. He spurs his mount to a trot and then lopes away as Adeline stoically watches the horseback figure's westward departure. She raises her hand to wave, then fights the strong impulse and slowly drops it to her side. The mounted rider stays on course to join the others in the wheeled carriage, as they crest over the hill on the horizon.

~*~

Beyond the edge of town, the sun settles among big, colorful clouds in the evening sky as the day comes to a close. Along the road, the worker packs his construction materials and gathers his tools of the carpentry trade. He steps aside from the newly created town sign, which reads;

~ Adeline ~
West Texas, Presidio County

The End.

Eric H. Heisner is an award-winning writer, actor and filmmaker. He is the author of several Western and Adventure novels: *West to Bravo, Seven Fingers a' Brazos, T. H. Elkman, Africa Tusk* and *Wings of the Pirate*. He can be contacted at his website:

www.leandogproductions.com

Ethan Julio Pro was born in 2001 to a multi-talented and creative family. Raised in Santa Clarita, California he showed an affinity for the arts at a very young age and demonstrated a natural skill well beyond his years. Continuing with his artistic gift, he aims to follow in his father's footsteps with a career as a professional artist.

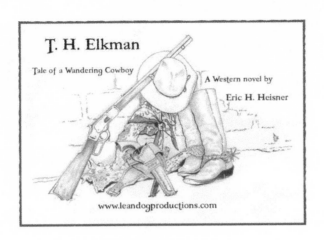

T. H. Elkman

Tale of a Wandering Cowboy

A Western novel by

Eric H. Heisner

www.leandogproductions.com

WEST TO BRAVO

A Western Novel

By Eric H. Heisner

WWW.LEANDOGPRODUCTIONS.COM

Wings of the Pirate

A high-flying Adventure Novel

By Eric H. Heisner

Limited time pre-order at:

www.inkshares.com

illustrations by

Al P. Bringas

www.leandogproductions.com

CPSIA information can be obtained
at www.ICGtesting.com
Printed in the USA
LVHW091627190720
661084LV00005B/262/J